ASSASSIN'S MENACE

ASSASSIN'S MAGIC 3

EVERLY FROST

Frost, Everly
Assassin's Menace

For information on reproducing sections of this book or sales of
this book, go to
www.EverlyFrost.com
everlyfrost@gmail.com

For everyone who carries books in their pockets, bags, and hearts.

CHAPTER ONE

I step inside the warm café, inhaling the scent of mocha lattes and freshly baked muffins, my favorite combination. If only I were here to eat them. I quickly head past the neat tables and sing out "Good morning" to Joe, the café's owner. I hang up my coat and swap it for the blueberry-colored waitressing apron with my nametag attached to it: *Grace.*

It's not my real name. I don't use my real name anymore.

I love that the apron has two wide, deep pockets at the front: one to contain my order notebook and the other … I grin as I slip a new hardcover book from my coat into my apron. It's heavy and drags the apron down on that side, but I love the weight. Books are the only things I splurge on, what I save my pennies for. It reminds me that at the end of the day there's something good waiting for me.

I check my watch: six a.m. The morning crowd is just starting to drag themselves in, eyes half open, begging for coffee. I hurry out to help Joe and take orders from the customers who want breakfast. Most of them are regulars and I know their orders like I know the first lines of my favorite books.

Joe catches me checking my watch as I join him behind the counter. He gives me a proud smile. "You're always on time, Grace."

I return his smile. He's a great boss, but the truth is … I'm not sure how much longer I can work here. I've already stayed way longer than I planned. While I work, I remain conscious of my surroundings, what's going on outside the shop as well as inside it. It's an old habit, one I can't get rid of.

Outside the shop window, an old lady in a tattered coat pauses briefly before quickly moving on. She's homeless and makes most people uncomfortable—and she knows it—so she doesn't stick around. I'm not sure how she survived the particularly frosty winter. At the end of the day, I'll put together a paper plate of the random muffins and pastries that nobody else wants and leave it at the side of the front step for her. Joe knows I do it, but he's never tried to stop me.

The old lady glances back as if she's checking something behind her and then disappears beyond the window at the same moment as a couple runs along the sidewalk. They stop directly in front of the café and jog on the spot.

I haven't seen them before. The girl looks like a college student; she's tall, slender, and brunette. Her hair is drawn up into a rough ponytail, but the color and cut tell me she paid a million dollars for that hairstyle. Expensive phone clipped to her waist. Expensive running shoes. Definitely from money.

The guy is older and he's … massive … all muscle, with striking, almost-black brown hair that is long on top and short at the sides. They're both wearing sports gear, probably thermal, but short-sleeved. *Seriously? In this weather?* It hasn't turned spring in Boston and it's freezing outside—or *crisp* as I like to think of it, because it feels less cold to describe it that way. Just looking at those two makes my toes turn numb.

A sleek, black car pulls up into the parking bay outside and the girl waves to the driver. That would explain why they're happy to run around outside without coats: a warm car waits for them as soon as they finish exercising.

I refocus on my task, taking the order of a customer at the table nearest to the window, but in the next moment the bell jingles above the door.

It's hard not to stare as the girl enters the shop, framed by the larger male behind her. He looms in the doorway, a protective force. They pause in the entrance as if they expect to be swarmed by a mob. I don't think they're movie stars, but the guy does seem familiar to me.

The girl half-turns back to him, her lips curving, murmuring, "See, I told you it would be fine. C'mon, they have the best milkshakes here. You can't leave Boston before you have one."

His shrug turns into a grin. His raised eyebrows say he's too old to be ordering kid's food. His deep voice carries the slightest southern accent as he says, "Milkshakes, huh?"

"Hey, we missed out on each other's childhoods. We have a lot of catching up to do."

There's a striking resemblance between them. They don't quite have the same hair color, but definitely the same eyes: green with stunning blue rims. At first glance they looked like a couple, but now I'm thinking brother and sister—especially after the comment about their childhood.

She tugs on his arm and he strides after her, retaining his protective loom over her while he assesses the room. I narrow my eyes at the way he quickly studies the exits, counts the customers, runs his eye over all the items in the room that could be used as a weapon, all in a practiced casual manner that nobody else would notice. It's like watching a mirror image of my own behavior.

Except that I stopped checking the exits about a

month ago. I've definitely stayed too long, got too comfortable. I sigh inwardly. I thought I had a reason to stick around, but it turns out I was wrong about that.

They choose a table in the middle on the left side. The other wait staff are late, so it's up to me to serve them. I take a deep breath as I approach. The girl is talking about her college major, and her brother—if that's what he is—seems happy to listen. He may hide his other reactions, but it's clear he adores her.

When she pauses and looks up, I ask, "May I take your order?"

True to her promise—and her brother's amusement—she orders two milkshakes. Before I can move away, she says, "Oh, hey, what are you reading?"

I glance down at my pocket, surprised she noticed the book peeking out of it. She may not be as reserved as her brother, but she's just as observant. I slide the book out into the open so she can see the title before I let it drop back into my pocket.

She asks, "Is it any good?"

"I haven't started it yet. I hope so."

She turns back to her brother with a smile. "Do you read, Cain?"

"Not as much as I'd like to, Parker." Cain's gaze sweeps across me as he speaks. It looks like a casual gesture, but he's doing it to someone who recognizes the behavior.

In one glance he's sized up my height, weight, the chocolate smudge on my apron, my blond hair, my nametag, and my chewed fingernails. Yep, I'm twenty years old and I still chew my nails. It's the one nervous tic I allow myself to have. I quietly curl the ends of my fingers behind my notebook to hide them, making a mental note that it's time to kick the habit.

Parker shakes her head at Cain. "You should find time, big brother."

I find myself smiling. There's something contagious about Parker's lighthearted smile. I ask, "Would you like to order anything else?"

"Two plates of bacon and eggs, sunny side up, please." She laughs when Cain gives her a surprised look. She says, "You thought I was going to order egg whites, didn't you? We just ran two miles. I'm not afraid to eat."

I jot down their order and glance up as the bell rings again, but it's not a customer. It's Jeremy and Sophie, the other two wait staff. I exhale and force myself to relax. Until a week ago, Jeremy and I were dating. I fell for his deep brown eyes and easygoing personality. He was the reason my intended three-month stay turned into six months. He was my first for many things—too many things—and now I'm determined that he'll be my last. There's no point pretending I can have a normal relationship when I can't tell anyone my name.

I never should have come back to Boston in the first place.

Jeremy doesn't acknowledge me, sauntering past with Sophie close beside him. It's hard to miss the way he squeezes her butt as they round the corner into the coatroom.

Wow, he moved on fast.

"Hey." Parker reaches out to gain my attention. She's going to ask me why I haven't taken their order to the kitchen yet. How can I just stand here gawking while they're waiting for their food?

Before I can apologize, she says the most surprising thing. Her voice and expression are gentle and genuine. "Are you okay?"

I'm stunned. I can't remember the last time someone asked me that, let alone a complete stranger. I shake myself. Remind myself I'm tougher than this. "Sorry. Yes. I'll be back with your food."

I deliver their order to the kitchen staff. I've already taken all the other prepared orders out to the required tables, so I steal a moment to gather myself, leaning up against the wall in the nook between the coat room and the kitchen.

So Jeremy broke my heart. So what? I'll get over it and remember not to open my heart again.

Then I suddenly realize that my current location is the last place I should be. The coatroom is where Jeremy and Sophie went and they're taking their time coming back out. Jeremy's familiar voice wafts out to me. "Last night was incredible."

There's a long pause. Are they kissing? Sophie gives an exaggerated moan-sigh. "I don't know why you wasted so much time on Grace."

"God, yeah. She's got nothing on you, babe. You are amazing."

That's what he'd said to me. That I was beautiful. That I was amazing.

I feel like I've been doused in ice water. My whole body just went numb. It's my own fault. I never should have stayed. I never should have believed I could have something normal. I'm the daughter of a criminal—I don't get to be normal.

I spin, trip, and bump over someone standing right behind me. My defensive training kicks in. I'm not athletic, not by a long shot, but I always had quick reflexes. I can move fast when I want to. I grab the guy's shoulders to keep my balance, but to my surprise he's faster, catching me and bending his knees slightly at the same time so he doesn't knock the wind out of me.

He draws me upright and I find myself hard up against his chest. I can't even draw breath. It's like the wind was knocked out of me. I can sense … all of him … every muscle in his arms cradling my back, every flex in his thigh, every ripple in his chest. His hands grip either side of my waist to steady me, and the way his palms flex against the curve at the top of my hips stops the breath in my lungs.

My gaze jolts upward to Cain's face. His quick inhale tells me he's as surprised as I am. Startled green eyes like the color of a stormy sea meet mine. Up this close, I can see the bristles shadowing his jawline as if he meant to shave but didn't have time.

What was he doing so close behind me? And what is going on with my heart right now? And ... *oh no* ... did he hear what Jeremy and Sophie said about me?

I'm beyond embarrassed. I never understood the desire to leap into a hole in the ground, but right now I wish I could disappear.

He doesn't seem in any hurry to release me. His gaze softens. "Are you okay?"

I find myself speaking the truth. "I'm not having a very good day."

Whoa, where did that come from? Honesty about my feelings has never been my forte. And why does he care?

"Well..." he says, adjusting me so I'm standing on my own two feet, releasing me and putting a stop to all those head-spinning sensations. "At least you won't be without a pen."

He holds it up for me. I must have left it on the table. He came to return it.

There's a gasp behind me and I jolt to see Sophie

and Jeremy gaping in the doorway that leads into the coatroom.

Sophie's jaw drops. She squeals, "Oh, my God. It's Cain Carter!"

It takes me a moment to catch up. Cain Carter...

Now I know why he seems familiar. His name has been plastered all over magazines and online news sites over the last few months: Cain Carter, Boston's youngest and most ambitious businessman. At twenty-one years of age he's already worth upwards of something in the high millions.

According to the magazines piled on the table in the corner of the café, he grew up in the South and relocated here a few months ago for reasons unknown. I'm guessing it might have something to do with his sister. But if the tabloids haven't gotten wind of her existence yet, then no wonder he and Parker were cautious about being seen together in public.

I take a step back so I have a clear line of sight into the café to locate Parker. She's peering in our direction. It takes her two seconds to realize they've been made. The disappointment on her face is heartbreaking. I guess she doesn't get to have "normal" either.

Cain's expression turns to stone. "Looks like I have to go, after all." For a moment, his expression softens. "Have a better day, Grace."

Then he swings away from me, strides toward

Parker, throws a hundred dollar bill down on the table, and whisks her out the door.

Feeling like I'm made out of wood, I follow his footsteps. Outside, the car door slams and the vehicle disappears. I pick up the cash and take it to Joe. He runs it through the register and gives me the leftover amount after Cain and Parker's meals are paid for.

He grins. "That's some tip."

I look from the money to the spot where Cain caught me, and then past it to Jeremy. He has the grace to look embarrassed. He's smart enough to know that I overheard him.

This is one chapter in my life I'm putting behind me.

"I'll take two muffins and two mocha lattes, thanks, Joe," I say, pulling off my apron and placing it on the counter. "And then I'm afraid I have to quit."

Joe sighs. "I knew I'd lose you one day. If you need a reference, let me know. I'll gladly give you one."

"Thanks."

I retrieve my coat and shoulder bag, put my book into the inner pocket where it rests against my side, and pay Joe for the food. I wrap my scarf around my neck and chin, pull up my hood, and exit the café juggling two lattes and two brown paper bags.

I head to the last place I saw the old homeless lady. It's time to share a meal with her. She usually sticks to

the alleyways during the day, so she should be somewhere nearby. I peer down one alley, then another.

The street is lined with electricity poles, dotted
with old flyers in all colors. Ten minutes later, I reach
the quieter end of the long street and I'm worried I'll
have to give up. I really wanted the lady to have a
warm drink for once. One sip of my latte tells me it's
getting cold. I stop and lean against the nearest pole,
trying to avoid the trash can beside it.

One of the flyers catches my attention, mostly
because it's the same blueberry color as my waitressing apron. In bold black lettering, it says:

*Feeling lost? Find yourself in books. The Tomb Bookshop
is hiring now.*

I need a job and I have customer service experience. Working in a bookstore would be a dream for
me. There's something comforting about being
surrounded by so many worlds hidden in pages,
worlds I can escape to. The flyer looks old though.
They're bound to have hired someone by now. Still, I
take it down and shove it in my pocket, just in case I
change my mind.

A clatter from the next alleyway draws my attention. I pick up my pace in the direction of the sound. A
muffled gasp meets my ears as I round the corner and
peer down the lane. It's wider than most, lined with
trash cans. One of them lies on its side, garbage bags
strewn across the pavement, and next to them...

The old homeless lady leans on her side, gripping the arms of a man in a mask, who is holding her by the throat.

What the...? He's choking her!

It doesn't occur to me to back the hell away and call for help. She'll be dead by the time someone with authority appears on the scene. It also doesn't occur to me to run for my life. Big guys in masks don't scare me. They probably should, but I grew up surrounded by them, got desensitized by all the violence, so I don't feel fear. I drop my bag at the alleyway entrance and pitch one of the coffee cups at his back to get his attention.

He jerks as the cup splashes liquid across his shoulders. He loosens his hold on the lady's throat long enough for her to scoot away from him, gasping for breath as she rubs her neck. She looks for a place to escape, but she's got nowhere to go. The alley is a dead end. I'm standing in the only exit and her would-be killer is between her and me.

Her assailant draws up to his full height to face me, fully clad in black: pants, shirt, boots, and a full face-mask. Only his hands are visible. And his eyes—amber with chocolate flecks. I read all the emotions in them, the dominant ones being surprise and annoyance.

I don't waste time with words. Talking isn't going to save her life. I throw the other coffee cup straight at his face. He bats it away with his fist so that it hits the grimy brick beside him. Caramel liquid splatters across the pavement.

He growls, low and deep, in a way that tells me I've made him mad.

With a quick movement, he draws back his arm and releases a sharp object right at me. The dagger thuds into the wall of the wooden building, beside my face.

I don't scream. I'm not a screamer. I stopped screaming when I was thirteen years old and Dad put a gun in my hands and told me to fucking shut up and shoot.

I drop the bags of muffins, but not because I'm scared. I need my hands to be free. The dagger quivers beside my face. It has two letters etched on it in large silver script right at my eye level: *SL*.

What does that stand for? *Super Large?* Seems like the sort of acronym a guy would use. Either this man has bad aim or that was a warning shot. He turns back to the old woman as if he's certain I'll run away now. She tries to get away as he grabs her once more by the throat, but he pauses when he realizes I'm not going anywhere.

He inclines his head sharply back the way I came as if he thinks I might be stupid. Don't I understand he wants me to leave? The dagger was a message. A warning. His gesture says: *Get the hell out of here. This is not your business.*

Like hell it's not.

I have no idea what "SL" stands for. If I'm supposed to be frightened, I'm not. I wrench the dagger from the wall and grip it in my fist, adjusting it for maximum leverage. My knife skills are rusty but they'll come back to me.

My heartbeat slows; a powerful calm takes over. It was always this way. Every time Dad gave me a weapon, every time I held a dagger or a gun, everything got really slow, really serene.

I am completely in control.

I'll get the shakes when it's all over, but for now the whole world may as well be at peace.

I stride toward the lady's assailant, judging his strengths and weaknesses from his height and build, assessing the way he's using his hands—brute strength—to subdue her. Another dagger is clipped onto his belt, out in the open, which means it's up for grabs like the one I'm holding now.

Knife fights are quick and brutal. They get messy fast. Unlike the assailant, I have decreased motion because of my clothing. My old man's coat is thick and warm. It's the only thing Dad left me—literally the coat off his back—it's not designed for a fight. I'm not taking it off though. Together with my hood and scarf, I could be anyone. He won't be able to identify me.

Actually … he might not realize I'm a woman. No lady I know would be caught dead in this coat. It

EVERLY FROST

completely hides my curves, but I refuse to give it up. I might have gone through stages of hating my dad, but this is the only thing I have left of him.

Now, I have to use every second wisely.

The man's eyes widen as he realizes I'm not going away. For a moment he looks at me as if he thinks I'm walking toward him simply to return his dagger. I keep it raised in my fist, pointed to the right, a fighting grip. His gaze flicks to it and he jolts a little.

Any fighter worth his salt will recognize the way I'm holding it, along with the message I'm sending: *I'm coming for you.*

He's so surprised he lets me get within arm's reach before he reacts.

I slash right at his face. It's a warning swipe more than anything else. I don't want to kill him. I just want him to leave the lady alone. I'm not sure if he'll feel the same way toward me though. If this guy is prepared to kill a harmless old woman, he won't have any problem ending me.

He drops the lady so he's free to grab his spare knife.

She scrambles away from him, scooting up against the back of the alleyway as he rounds on me. I leap backward when he takes a swipe at my stomach, a slashing cut that would have run from one side of my torso to the other ... if he was serious about it.

His attack was a test swing too. He wants to check

16

my reflexes and determination, to find out if I pose a real challenge. My nimble evasion just told him I'm not going down easily.

"Who are you?" he asks, his voice muffled behind his mask.

I don't answer. My voice will give away that I'm female, and I'm determined to take my ruse to the bitter end.

He makes a swift swipe at my face, but I duck, arms up so that if I'm not quick enough he'll cut my forearms and not my face. At the same time, I grab his knife hand, push it wide, and kick my foot into his stomach, following up with a quick uppercut to his jaw. I use my left hand, not my knife hand, so it doesn't have the same impact, but even so, his knife flies wide as he goes down.

He leaps back to his feet just as fast, quicker than I anticipated for such a big guy. I narrowly evade a hit to my temple, landing a punch to his side instead. When I try to knee him, he pushes my leg down and forces me off balance. It's my turn to hit the ground, rolling out of the way as he comes after me. He stomps the spot where I'd lain a split second ago.

I end up right beside his fallen dagger, snatching it up as I find my feet and turn to face him again.

Now I have both weapons.

Before I can use them, he darts up between my arms and tries to grab my scarf to reveal my face, but he only succeeds in drawing it further up over my nose. I've tied it securely around my neck and mouth to stay warm. It takes him a second to figure out my scarf isn't going anywhere.

But before I leap backward, he throat punches me instead.

Uh...

I gasp, stumble backward, but I still have both knives. It's no use trying to get him to back off. I use the motion to my advantage, pivoting, spinning, and slashing each dagger, one after the other across his chest. The blades slice against his suit but don't cut through.

It's my turn to get a case of the wide eyes.

His suit protects him. I don't have anything near that advantage. I abandon the gentle approach, following up my swinging slashes with another boot to his chest, following him as he stumbles backward, taking advantage of his failing balance to slam the dagger into his shoulder. The knife glances off his chest, shuddering in my hand.

He winces.

I've bruised him, but it didn't break through the material. Shock shatters my calm for the first time.

That's some serious protective gear.

Before I can blink, he slides another weapon from his boot and rams it upward. The new knife thuds right into my side, aimed to slide between my ribs. It sticks and stops. I inhale, swallow a scream, fear crashing through me as I jerk upright and wobble backward.

He glares at me, rising to his feet, waiting for me to fall.

But ... I don't feel any pain.

I'm not dead. I don't feel a cut. There's no blood.

Maybe I'm in shock and I can't feel anything.

Maybe he missed me?

Nope. The knife is sticking out of me, attached to my side. I steady myself. If I'm dying, I'm taking this guy down with me.

His suit is made of material and that means it has seams.

I leap back at him, abandoning my fear and angling the knife to the side, slicing down the side seam as I pass by. His suit splits open, exposing his stomach, all muscles.

A glow grows around his edges that makes it hard for me to focus on him, but I head right back into the fight, spinning and kicking him so hard that he slams against the brick behind him.

I land on him, pressing my blade to his bare stomach.

He freezes.

Fear and confusion dance in his eyes.

"How did you...?" He shakes it off and demands again, "Tell me who you are!"

My vocal chords are lacerated because of the punch he landed to my throat. I'm sick of hiding my true identity. It's time this asshole knows who he's dealing with.

My voice rasps, scratchy, a deep growl. "My name … is Archer Ryan."

My real name. The one I don't tell anyone.

His eyes widen with shock. He recognizes my name.

Good. He should be afraid.

My dad was Patrick Ryan, one of the most feared mobsters in Boston before he went down in a blaze of glory, taking ten hit men with him on his way to hell. Or so the story goes. Seven of them were actually my kills, but that didn't save him.

I couldn't save him.

That old bastard, he dressed me as a boy, cut my hair short, taught me how to use every weapon imaginable, and told everyone he had a son. When I reached puberty, he made me wear baggy clothing and strap my chest and waist to disguise my curves. That only worked for a year—until I developed a D cup to be exact. After that, I hid in the shadows, became a name, a myth, someone who was never seen. Anyone who saw my face or figure didn't live long enough to talk about it. Even the nanny who raised me disappeared and I had no doubt Dad was responsible. His answer to everything was a bullet. I hated him for my solitude, but I came to understand his motives as I got older.

In the world of crime, sons are allies. Daughters are liabilities.

Judging by the shock on my assailant's face, being the child of a well-known mobster gives me an advantage.

I press the knife against his stomach, drawing blood but not enough to kill him. "Get off my turf before I end you."

He splays his hands wide, sliding upward, finding his feet, placing each step carefully. I let him go, wary in case it's a trick on his part.

He makes it to the fire escape at the side of the building and steps onto the bottom rung, but right before he disappears up it, he says, "You don't know what you've done, Archer Ryan."

I let the threat wash over me. Most men will use threats to save face when they've been beaten. I shrug it off as he disappears up and over the edge of the roof. My biggest concern now is the dagger that didn't kill me...

As soon as I'm certain that the man is gone, I check the knife he thrust into my side, holding my breath. I'm not sure what I'll find. The dagger is rammed into something ... but not the ribs he aimed for.

I almost laugh when I discover that it's stuck in my hardcover book.

Well, what do you know? Reading just saved my life. I cycle through amazement, relief, and then rage as I assess the damage to my beautiful possession. That asshole's dagger sliced all the way to the back cover; every page has a slit in it. It's unnerving that he had that kind of strength. I recall the strange glow that grew around him, like an electrified force.

I shake it off as I deposit his dagger safely into my pocket, on the outside of the book so there's no chance I'll stab myself with it when I move around. Then I reach for the old lady, helping her to her feet. She doesn't cry or go into shock. She's tough—I'll give her that. But her eyes are wide pools.

Her hands hover across her damaged throat as she whispers, "Archer Ryan."

Yeah. That's me. Apparently my parents wanted to give me a strong name. At least, that's what Dad told me. I don't remember Mom.

It looks like this lady recognizes my name too. Except, unlike her would-be killer, she knows I'm female because she's seen me come and go in this coat day after day.

My voice is still husky as I ask her, "Who was that guy?"

Her voice is lacerated like mine. "His name is Lutz Logan. He is an assassin."

I frown, brushing off her fearful reply. "Assassins are myths."

She shakes her head, pointing to my pocket where the dagger hides. "He belongs to Slade's Legion."

That explains the "SL," but I struggle to believe her. I believe in mobsters. I believe in hit men whose job it is to kill and bury their boss's rivals. I believe in thugs, criminals, and drug lords. I believe in tyrants like the newest queen of the underground—a woman who calls herself Lady Tirelli.

I believe in acts of vengeance and blood feuds.

But assassins are something else entirely—trained warriors who disappear into the shadows, who hire themselves out to deal death purely for money. They don't exist. Besides, why would anyone pay to kill this old lady?

I try to refocus the conversation. "You know my name but I don't know yours."

"I'm Briar."

"I'm really sorry about the coffee, Briar, but I brought you some food. You must be hungry." I gesture back along the alleyway but my smile slips when she grabs my arm before I can move further. Her bony grip is surprisingly strong.

She speaks urgently. "Archer Ryan, you need to run."

"Why? Because of that thug?" He threatened that I would regret my actions, but most men do after you beat them in a fight.

"Slade's Legion will hunt you down. You interfered

in a sanctioned assassination. They follow a code. They don't tolerate interference. Especially not from someone who can beat Lutz Logan."

I contemplate her. She didn't scream or cry when the guy was choking the life out of her. Not when I fought him either, but now tears spring into her eyes.

She says, "I don't believe you are the person the stories say you are. I don't want you to die because of me, Archer Ryan."

I shrug. "If they're going to hunt me, then nowhere is safe."

Even Dad had nowhere to hide in the end. There was only one woman he trusted—a woman I never met. He called her his "Glass Fox." They died on the same night. As soon as she was killed, that was the end of him.

Briar points to my side. I have no idea why—I already removed the dagger—until a flap of blue paper catches my eye. It's the flyer that was pasted on the pole out on the street. It must have worked its way out of my pocket during the fight.

Briar says, "Go to the Tomb."

"A bookstore?" I'm dubious now. Sure, I love to escape into books, but realistically a bookstore isn't going to save me.

She pulls me closer. Her voice is raspy, forced, the damage to her vocal chords revealing itself. "Go to the Tomb. You will be safe there."

Safe in a Tomb. Sounds perfectly likely.

Briar's gaze darts around the alleyway. The shadows suddenly seem deeper. The street outside is too quiet. An uneasy tension settles in my stomach. Whether or not I believe that my assailant is coming back to take revenge, I have a very strong sense that I need to get out of here right now.

I spin back to her. "What about you?"

She gives me a toothy grin and whispers, "Once an assassination fails, the target is off limits. They only get one shot. You saved my life. But your own is in danger. Go now, Archer Ryan."

I find it strange that she keeps calling me by both my names. But it's clear that Briar really wants me go to this bookstore. Truth be told, I'm a little uneasy now. Whether or not I believe that assassins exist, that guy was serious about killing Briar. Dark bruises are already spreading across her throat where he wrapped his big hands. He wasn't a hallucination and I've got his dagger to prove it.

I need to get out of here but going to a bookstore isn't my best bet—no matter how insistent Briar is. I make no promises as I head to the alleyway's opening. Once I'm at the corner, I peer around it. The street is too quiet. Too deserted. I glance back one last time. "I hope you'll…"

I was going to tell her I hoped she'd be okay, but she's already in the process of darting past me.

"I'll intercept them," she says, racing away down the street in the opposite direction to the bookstore.

Taking one last look at the flyer scrunched in my hand, I shove it into my pocket and out of sight.

I need to go back to my apartment before the shakes kick in. The after-effects of fighting are what I fear—my body shuts down and I'll be completely vulnerable. It's like punishment for being so calm while I fight—I feel the fight afterward, not during.

I will be able to recover safely once I reach my apartment. Then I'll get my things and catch the next bus out of here. I only paid up this week's rent so it's not a big loss. I have enough money left from Cain's tip to pay for the bus ticket.

It's time to leave Boston once and for all.

CHAPTER TWO

I'm only halfway up the street, just approaching the café again, when the shock hits me.

Too soon! It has never hit me this fast after a fight. I usually have an hour at least. I stumble across the pavement, my legs wobbling and my eyesight blurring.

No, please, no. I can't collapse here.

I try to right myself before I draw attention from people passing by. I take deep breaths, fighting off the darkness encroaching on my vision.

I don't have to look back to know I'm being followed. A cute guy in faded jeans, leather jacket, and blue scarf peeled off the far corner as soon as I appeared on the street again. He looks like a college student, clean cut and harmless. But he's been on my six for the last five minutes. He's got something up his sleeve too; he's not smart enough to stop checking it. It could be a dagger. Or a syringe containing a paralytic if kidnapping is his game.

I was reckless to speak my real name aloud. I have no way of knowing whether the guy following me is working for someone with a long-held grudge against my dad or whether he's involved in this assassin stuff that Briar was so worried about.

It doesn't matter. He's gaining on me.

If I collapse, I'll be defenseless.

Part of me wants to turn around and face him right now before I'm totally gone. It's not like me to run from a fight. But now I'm really shaking, my hands clattering against my sides, my shoulders trembling. I estimate I have five minutes at most before I literally pass out.

Keep moving, Archer. Don't forget the dagger in your pocket. I don't want to reach for it and give away that I still have it, but if I become desperate, I will. I have to believe that the calm will return once I hold it in my hand again.

I stick to the populated pathways, walking near people at all times: a couple holding hands strolling down the path, then a group of girls…

Once I pass the café, the shakes become unbearable. My heart is pounding. I'm sweating despite the cold. I need to sit down. I need to lie down.

I bump into the next person—a guy—and he reaches out to steady me.

"Grace? Are you okay?"

Oh no. The last thing I need right now is to meet someone I know. I just need to get back to my apartment. I don't need anyone's help. I wobble as I look up, making a mockery of my own determination not to lean on him.

I stare in shock. "Cain?"

He assesses me with eyes that remind me of a stormy sea. He's still dressed in workout gear, but I don't see Parker anywhere nearby. I'm surprised Cain recognizes me given that I'm covered up to my ears. Only my eyes and cheekbones are visible. I make another mental note to switch up my contact lenses. The blue ones I currently use are too pretty, too eye-catching. Using contact lenses with such a memorable color is clearly not doing me any favors.

"You're shaking. What's wrong?" His grip tightens on my arms and I'm shocked to realize that my legs just failed. He's the only reason I'm standing upright.

And … *dammit* … he knows it.

My voice is small. The admission hurts much more than the fact that I'm completely reliant on a stranger right now. "I don't feel very well."

That's twice today he's ripped the truth out of me.

He glances to his left, where a black sedan waits, his speech cautious. "Okay … so … getting into a car with a stranger is normally a really bad idea and I would absolutely tell you not to do it, but I don't think I can leave you here."

His driver has parked the vehicle in the parking bay again. Parker isn't inside it. I pretend for a moment that I'm not completely reliant on Cain right now. "What are you doing back here?"

His expression hardens. "I sent Parker home and then I came back to pay off your friends so they wouldn't talk to the press."

A trickle of indignation finds its way back into my body. "They aren't my friends. Well, maybe Joe is. Jeremy and I *used* to date, but I use the past tense with emphasis…"

My voice trails off. As I speak, Cain focuses on something behind me, his attention shifting from me for the first time since he stopped me from falling. I attempt to turn to see what he's looking at.

The guy who was tailing me stands only five paces away, but he stops in the middle of the pathway. He considers Cain with an uneasy expression. If I wasn't so out of it already, I'd say he was worried.

Cain's eyes narrow.

That's all it takes for the guy to back away. He makes it look casual. Then he turns and strides down the street, pulling out his cell phone as he walks. So it was a phone up his sleeve after all. He's too far away for me to hear what he says.

My head tips back. *Oh God, no ... I can't control my limbs. I'm going to ... pass out...*

Cain's grip ascends to the back of my head. With one hand he deftly slips off my hood, and with the other he supports my head before it tips backward, all without letting me fall. Unearthly tingles shoot down my spine from the places where his fingertips rest against my scalp.

He murmurs into my ear: "I need to get you out of here right now."

My heart almost stops when his lips brush my ear. I tell myself it's the oncoming disintegration of my senses. My knees are already jelly. His husky voice has nothing to do with it...

Somehow, the touch of his hand on my head keeps me grounded and present. The threatening darkness recedes, but only enough that I don't fall unconscious right then.

Despite the certainty in his voice, there's a question in it. *Am I okay with that?*

If I hadn't seen him with Parker this morning, there's no way I would get into a car with him, no matter how much money the tabloids say he has. He could be a millionaire serial killer for all I know. But the reality right now is that if he lets me go, I'll end up passed out on the sidewalk. That's not a safe option either. Especially since I have no doubt my pursuer will come back.

Even if I don't believe in assassins, there's something going on here. Of the two options, I'll take the guy with the sweet sister who is offering to help me out.

I mumble, "Okay. But take me to my apartment, please."

He frowns. "I think you need a doctor…"

"No hospitals!" The assertion saps the last of my energy. Hospitals require identification, and then medical staff go digging where they shouldn't.

Dad's orders repeat on me: *You fix your own wounds or you fucking die from them.*

He taught me how to disinfect and stitch cuts, even how to remove bullets. Besides, I'm not going to die from my current ailment. I just need to lie down for half an hour…

Cain is reluctant. "Okay. Please tell my driver where to go and he'll take us there."

"Thank you."

As soon as he has my agreement, he lifts me up, hooking one arm under my knees and supporting my head and back with his other. His driver jumps out of the car, no doubt waiting for such a sign, and races around to the passenger door to open it for us.

Cain leverages me inside the vehicle onto the back seat as if I don't weigh a thing—which I know isn't true. I may be able to bust a move once I have a weapon in my hand, but I'm taller than average and curvy in a lot of places.

Leaving the door open for a moment, Cain speaks rapidly with his driver in hushed tones before he closes the door and rounds the front of the vehicle.

He uses the other door to slide into the seat next to me, brushing the hair out of my eyes to check me over, his expression becoming increasingly worried when I can't focus on him.

His question is direct, "What happened?"

"I had a run-in with an..." I squint at him. Frown. *I'm not saying "assassin" aloud. I'll sound ridiculous.*

"With who, Grace?"

My voice slurs. Without the touch of his hand on my head, the world sways as the vehicle backs out of the parking space.

I won't remain conscious for long and there's nothing I can do to stop the oncoming darkness. "Big guy ... knife ... old lady ... stopped him ... need to ... sleep..."

I slide toward Cain and my head lolls onto his shoulder and settles there.

He doesn't seem to mind.

He strokes my falling hair out of my closing eyes and murmurs under his breath. "What have you got yourself into?"

That's all I hear before I pass out.

It feels like two seconds later that I revive inside the vehicle. Leaning on Cain's shoulder is like resting against a supercharged battery. My energy is back at a thousand percent and so is my sense of self-preservation.

I jolt away from him and slide across the leather seat until I'm pressed up against the far window. He remains where he is, giving me as much space as the back seat allows, keeping his tone moderated: "How are you feeling?"

As he speaks, his observant gaze takes in my eyes and posture. My alertness has the opposite effect that I thought it would: he relaxes instead of tensing up.

He says, "You look much better now. I was worried about you for a second there."

"I feel fine, thanks. I just needed a little nap." I know how odd that sounds, but I can't elaborate, because I have no explanation. Dad never helped me discover why I check out after a fight. He never took me to a doctor for answers. The only explanation I can come up with is a drastic adrenaline drop.

I consider our surroundings. "My place is in the opposite direction."

"I wasn't sure where we should go, so we've been driving around for the last minute in case you woke up. I was just about to take you to my doctor." Cain leans forward to the driver. "Can you turn the car around please? Grace will tell you where to go."

The driver glances at me in the rearview mirror, waiting for my instructions. I feel better that they are taking my wishes seriously.

I say, "Down this street for starters. Then take the second left."

I cringe a little. My apartment isn't exactly in a nice part of town. Still, I don't relax until it looks like he's doing exactly what I asked.

I attempt to exhale the tension from my body. It's warm in the car, and worse, under Cain's unwavering gaze I'm heating up with every passing moment.

I slip out of my jacket and pull off my scarf. At some point, I'll put my seatbelt on, but only once I'm sure I don't need to make a quick getaway...

"Grace!"

My eyes fly wide at the alarm in Cain's voice. "What?"

"There's a cut on your jaw."

I grimace. My opponent must have nicked it when he took a swipe at my face. Another weird thing about me: I don't feel pain so much. I'm aware of the injury, but it's more of a clinical awareness. I heal quickly, so it's never been much of a problem. "I'm sure I'll be fine."

Cain clearly disagrees. He leans toward me to examine it, lightly resting his thumb and forefinger beneath my chin to angle my face and study the wound. "It needs stitching."

My lips part at the unexpected tingles running from his fingertips down my neck and right into my heart. I try to find my voice. It's in there. Somewhere.

I manage, "I'm okay. Really."

He clears his throat. "I have a friend who says the same thing when she's hurt. It usually means she's not okay."

He doesn't elaborate, but his friend sounds like someone I'd get along with.

He purses his lips, deep in thought. A quick shake of his head indicates he isn't giving up. "With your permission, I'd like to have my doctor examine you. She's back at my house. I have an apartment in town, but the house is twenty minutes outside the city. She'll be able to look at the wound right away and stitch it if necessary."

"You have a personal doctor? She lives with you?" Maybe I shouldn't be surprised. Lifestyles of the rich and famous are foreign to me. I guess being a million-aire means he can keep a doctor on his payroll.

He lowers his hand, taking a little too long to answer. "I ... uh ... play a lot of sports." He shrugs. "Injuries are a regular part of my life. I have my own doctor so that I'm assured of privacy."

His sports excuse is bogus—I can tell by the way his tone changes as he speaks—but his need for privacy is real. I'm not sure how important his reasons should be to me. He could have a personal doctor for any reason. Parker could be sick. Cain could be dying. I halt my imagination before it gets out of control.

I hesitate to accept his help. It scares the stuffing out of me, not least because it means willingly heading into a foreign environment. But at the same time … nobody has ever offered to help me before. It's … nice … in a way that I wasn't expecting.

Also, stitching my own face is awkward.

I say, "You don't even know me."

He draws back. "You're right. We haven't been introduced." He holds out his hand to me across the space between us. "I'm Cain Carter, millionaire. I have a younger sister, Parker, who I only found out about a year ago." His expression becomes regretful. "And … I'm leaving Boston tonight."

Oh. For some reason, the leaving part is like a jab in my heart. But that's for the best. His doctor will take a look at me and then I'll never see him again. After all, I plan to leave today, too.

I swallow. It's my turn to introduce myself. "I'm … Grace Kennedy. Twenty years old. Not a penny to my name. Both parents dead and no siblings."

His expression softens at the whole orphan thing. It's not something I usually share, because I like to avoid the obvious question: *How did they die?*

I'm grateful when he doesn't ask. Instead, he leans

toward me again and the energy I sense from him is so strong it's almost unbearable.

"Now we know each other. Please accept my help, Grace." There's a question in his voice and eyes. And then a determined statement. "Your face is too perfect to let it scar. Not when I can do something about it."

I clear my throat, not sure how to take what I think is intended to be a cautious compliment. "Your doctor will need to have skills if you don't want that to happen."

He seems to take that as permission to angle toward the driver and take charge of the situation. "Sorry, Spencer, we need to turn around again. Can you take us back to the house?"

The driver gives him a nod in the rearview mirror. He takes all the changes of direction in stride.

Returning his attention to me, Cain says, "My doctor is a plastic surgeon, so there won't be any issues."

In the next breath he says, as if he knows it will ease my mind, "Parker is at the house. She's staying out of sight after this morning. She'll be happy to see you. It's not often she meets someone who carries books around like she does." His voice lowers, filling with regret again. "Which I didn't know until this morning."

He shakes himself. Glances at me as if he didn't mean to say that aloud.

I want to ask him about his relationship with his sister. He said he found out about her a year ago, but it's clear he only got to know her recently. I don't want to pry. Especially because I don't want him to think this was all some ploy to get information out of him. Sickos stalk famous people all the time. It occurs to me that he has as many reasons to be nervous about me as I do about him.

I decide I'm better off not talking. At some point he's going to want details about how I got the cut on my chin. I'm surprised he hasn't asked already.

I need to get my story straight in my head. I flush as I remember murmuring something about a big guy, a knife, and an old lady. An attempted mugging is my best explanation. As for passing out on his shoulder, I'll have to swallow my pride and pretend I fainted after the stress of the encounter.

Woe is me, I'm just a poor helpless female.

Ugh.

I fold my coat in my lap, winding it around my book and the knife that rests inside it, resting them both on top of my bag. The coat is too large to shove inside the small bag. Carrying a knife to someone's home isn't a great look, but there isn't much I can do about it now.

While we travel, Cain returns to his phone. The first call is to Parker. He says, "It's all sorted. I'm coming back." There's a pause. "Can you do me a favor? When the car arrives, come out the front. I'm bringing Grace with me and I think she'll feel better if you're there. Yes, Grace from the café." His eyes crinkle at the corners at whatever she said, his lips rising in a half smile. "Okay, Parker. You too."

Then he calls someone I'm assuming is the doctor even though he calls her by her first name—Sarah— before describing my wound to her. His tone is matter-of-fact as he tells her that I passed out as well.

The final call he makes is the shortest and most cryptic. What fascinates me the most is the way his whole demeanor changes. For a moment, I glimpse a different Cain, someone commanding and powerful in a way that sends shivers down my spine.

He growls a command to whoever picked up the line, "Report." There's a pause. "Right." Then: "Is every-thing ready? Good."

That's it. Conversation over. I focus on the view as silence descends around us.

Twenty minutes later, we've left the city behind and entered Weston, a place where the houses are mansions and the lawns are picture-perfect. A shudder runs down my spine. I came out this way once with Dad. He suspected his right-hand man was trying to undermine him—he was right. The guy had a house out this way and things got ugly fast. It was my first knife fight and not something I want to remember. It's lucky I don't scar easily or I'd have several nasty ones crisscrossing my back.

The car pauses at a tall security gate. An elegant wrought-iron fence runs the entire width of the property. It has an Old World look, but the modern security cameras aren't to be trifled with. No doubt the house has a hefty alarm system. I can't see behind the massive white mansion planted in the middle of the expansive lawn, but I assume the security behind the building is as complete as it is out the front.

Parker and another woman wait at the front of the house as the car pulls up. I quickly assess the property's exits. Now that the security gate is closed, I'll have to scale the fence if I want to get out of here...

I glance back at Cain to find myself under scrutiny. The slightly wary look in his eyes tells me he recognizes my behavior as quickly as I recognized his—he knows I'm assessing my surroundings for threats and escape routes.

I quickly hide my thoughts, clutching my bag and tucking my rolled-up coat under my arm as I get out of the vehicle. It's cold outside but I'm wary of unraveling my coat for the short walk to the door in case the knife drops out of it. I need to keep it out of sight at all costs.

Parker greets me with a shy smile. "Grace. Hi." She immediately checks out the cut on my chin. "Wow, that must hurt."

I bite my lip, not wanting to lie, opting for a noncommittal response. "It looks worse than it feels."

The woman dressed in a no-nonsense gray suit holds out her hand to me. "I'm Dr. Sarah Mathers. I'd like to take a look at you, if you don't mind?"

I guess it's straight to business, then.

Sarah leads me inside and Parker gives me a half smile. I try to place her age. Younger than me, maybe nineteen.

She says, "I'll see you when my overprotective brother deems you fit and healthy enough for a cup of hot chocolate."

Cain shrugs but Parker snags his arm as he passes, her smile disappearing. "I'm sorry about this morning. I thought it would be okay."

She bites her lip. Hard.

This morning I would have picked her as ultra-confident, but the girl I see now is vulnerable and genuinely worried.

He responds by instantly wrapping her up in a hug. "Hey, it's okay. Really. You're the one I'm trying to protect." He pulls back. Gives her a grin. "Luckily, greed is a good motivator. And I have dirt on every-one, so it's all good."

She relaxes. Then scoffs, "On everyone?"

His response is absolute. "Yes."

Parker diverts into a comfortable-looking lounge

room with a fireplace and plush chairs while Cain follows Sarah and me through the entrance, past the grand spiral staircase, through a corridor, and then another corridor. I almost lose track of how many times we turn a corner. This place is a maze for the unwary.

We finally reach a spacious room containing a surgical bed and a tray of instruments already prepared ... basically the perfect place to dispose of a body if you want to. Cain seems perfectly at home here, making me wonder how many times he's lain on this exact bed.

Color heats my cheeks. Beds and Cain ... not somewhere my mind should be going right now. Also unexpected. I'm done with men. Really I am.

Sarah asks me to put my coat and bag on the counter that extends all the way around three sides of the room, above which are cupboards with opaque glass doors. I reluctantly leave my coat on the counter before I sit on the edge of the surgical bed while she examines my wound.

She gives me a reassuring smile. "It should only take two stitches. You were lucky the attack wasn't lower or it would have cut your throat."

Like Cain, she doesn't ask me for details. I have a feeling those questions are being stored for later, and I'll do everything I can to avoid them.

I accept the local anesthetic she offers me and force

myself to lie still while she works over me. Cain pulls up a chair and sits quietly out of the way.

When the stitches are done, Sarah looks me in the eye. "Cain said you passed out."

My chin is numb from the anesthetic. I work my mouth a little, hoping the feeling wears off soon. I pretend to be embarrassed. "I think I fainted. It's not every day I intercept a mugging."

She tries a little harder. "There are further tests I can do to make sure you're okay."

"No." I try to soften my sharp response. "Thank you. I've always had naturally low blood pressure. A shock was all it took to make me pass out."

"Well, I won't do anything without your consent, so..." She turns and shrugs at Cain.

At some point he has relocated to the side of the room closest to the door. I frown at the fact that I didn't notice him do that. Just like I didn't sense him come up behind me this morning to return my pen. This man moves like a panther.

He says, "Thanks, Sarah. I'd like a minute alone with Grace now, please."

He folds his arms across his chest as she leaves the room.

I suck in a sharp breath at the change in his posture. Now that Sarah is gone, he isn't the protective older brother anymore, nor the polite employer, not even the arrogant millionaire, but someone much more dangerous...

In fact, he's starting to remind me of the guy in the alley ... what was his real name? Lutz something?

I slide off the bed, preparing to make an exit as quickly as I can, but before I reach my rolled-up coat on the opposite side of the room, Cain says, "A big guy, a knife, and an old lady."

For some reason, I don't want to lie to him. So I opt for half truths. I snatch up my coat, take a deep breath, and spin back to him, my expression deliberately blank. "Like I said to the doctor, I got in the way."

Cain levels his gaze with me. We're standing on opposite sides of the room, but his presence is somehow magnified despite the distance.

He says, "Here's what I know: Lutz Logan wasn't trying to rob Briar. He was trying to kill her. You stopped him and somehow disarmed him. I want to know how you did that."

My thoughts scatter and my stomach plummets. He knows Briar's name. He knows Lutz Logan. He knows that Lutz was trying to kill Briar, and now he's talking as if he knows I have the knife.

How? How? How? And what the hell am I going to do?

Cain lifts himself off the wall, unfolding his arms. "But what I really want to know is who you are."

An object glints in his fist.

Oh no...

I fight the impulse to freeze, patting my coat very

slowly, checking the location of the knife. My stomach sinks with every touch that confirms my fears.

The knife isn't where I left it.

Cain is holding it.

My brief vacation into a world where people take care of each other is over.

Now I have to fight for my life all over again.

CHAPTER THREE

*W*ithout taking my eyes off Cain, I re-balance my weight, settling into a defensive position, the coat and book held close to one side of my chest. A quick glance tells me that Sarah has unhelpfully cleaned away all the surgical instruments and the cupboards are locked. My only weapon is my book wrapped in my coat.

I don't know if Cain can fight or if his physique is all for show. I keep my eyes on his hands. The location of the knife is what's important now. I can fight without a weapon, but I'd prefer to be the one holding it. At the very least, I don't want to meet the sharp end of it.

His eyes widen.

Good. He recognizes the fighting stance I'm taking. That means he'll take me seriously.

His tone changes abruptly. "Easy, Grace. I just want answers."

I keep my breathing even and smooth. "You made a lot of statements. You didn't ask any questions."

His gaze flickers, no doubt in reflection. "You're right, I didn't."

He very slowly lifts the knife without making any sudden moves, turning it so that the hilt rests side-on in his large palm, making the etched initials visible to me.

Slade's damn Legion. Damn you, Slade, whoever you are.

Cain asks, "How did you disarm Lutz Logan?"

"That's like asking how someone wins a fight. I don't know how to answer except to give you a lesson in self-defense."

What I really hate is that he looks at me as if *I'm* the one who poses the danger. I guess he's thinking about Parker's safety. If I beat a guy like Lutz Logan, then I could hurt her, too.

I'm surprised by how frustrated and angry that makes me feel. As if I would hurt her. Or him. Or anyone actually. I never killed anyone who didn't try to kill me first. Archer Ryan may have had a violent reputation as a boy walking in his father's footsteps, but the stories and the reality were two different things.

Cain doesn't know any of that. In fact, he hasn't

mentioned my real name, so I'm guessing he doesn't know that part yet. All he knows is that he brought a dangerous stranger into his house who has the skills to beat a so-called assassin.

My emotions swing from indignation to anger and back again. Before I can retort, a dangerous grin grows on his face, accentuating the gorgeous angles of his jaw and mouth.

He says, "I'll take a demonstration."

Really? Is he spoiling for a fight?

I narrow my eyes at him. He's well and truly blocking the doorway. If I want to leave, I'm going to have to strong-arm him.

What really gets me is that I don't want to hurt him. Kindness is rare in my life, and for a few moments he gave it to me.

I grit my teeth. "Fine. Consider this a demonstration."

I stride toward him. He studies my approach, taking in my gait, the swing of my free arm, the way I'm gripping the book close to my chest. By the time I'm two paces away, his expression has become curious. I haven't made a move yet, haven't tried to throw anything, let alone a punch.

Right when he must think I'm not going to do anything more than walk straight at him, I flick the coat upward and outward, causing a visual block between us. I judge my throw perfectly. The book inside the pocket is perfectly placed at his head height. My closed fist darts out, connects with the book, and propels it right at his stunning face.

It would be a perfect hit … if he was still there.

He ducks at lightning speed, snatches the bottom of the coat out of the air, and pulls it with him as he swings and turns. He slams the door closed with his free hand at the same time.

A loud click tells me that it has an automatic lock. There's no visible handle on this side.

Oh, hell. My situation just got worse.

He's suddenly behind me.

His hand grazes my arm, the lightest touch tingling through me as I dance out of his reach, spinning to face him again.

He rolls up the coat, the book still inside it, and pegs it at the far wall, the furthest away from me as possible. All without taking his eyes off me. It slaps the wall and lands on the floor, a *thud* that sinks my heart.

We've switched positions. I'm now standing where he was and he is only two paces away. However … to my very great surprise, I spy the knife resting on the table next to me.

His gaze flicks to it, but not in a way that indicates he's going to make a grab for it.

He wants to make sure I see it.

He deliberately left it behind, but … why? Is he testing me?

I frown at him, trying to figure out his motives.

As much as I could use some calm right now, I don't pick it up. Instead, I take another swipe at him, this time with my foot so I can keep my distance. I put enough strength behind it to down him in an instant.

He easily evades the strike, his hand snapping around my ankle and pushing it down, pulling me forward as he steps toward me instead of pushing me away. I end up with my knee bent against his stomach, trying to balance on one leg, leaning into him. His arms wrap around my lower back, keeping me on my feet in an almost helpful gesture.

With a gasp I realize how closely our lower halves are pressed against each other, especially with my knee in the air.

He arches an eyebrow at me.

My scowl deepens.

I shove him away, thumping both fists toward his chest, which he evades with an agile twist of his torso. I fall forward, but I was ready for that, tucking my chin and rolling back to my feet. He's already there. One arm snakes around my waist from behind, but I spin again and his palm brushes all the way around my stomach and lower back as I glide out of his hold. Shivers run to my toes as his fingertips float across my torso.

I step backward, facing him, but now he goes on the offensive, pressing both palms against my shoulders, a firm grip. I let loose a rapid succession of blows with my fists, but he deftly evades all of them with lithe movements and *still* maintains hold of me. All while I'm stepping backward. It's the direction he seems to want me to go, which only makes me cranky.

I try again for a kick, even harder this time, but he moves at whirlwind speed, letting go of one of my shoulders, twisting just enough to avoid the blow, hooking his arm under my knee at the same time.

Damn, he's like liquid. No matter what I do, he rolls with it, and now ... I have nowhere to go.

I bump up against the wall, his arm still hooked under my leg, his palm resting against the outside of my thigh. His other hand presses against the top of my ribs, dangerously close to my breast.

My chest heaves, every inward breath narrowing the small gap between us. I count the blows I haven't landed: too many. In contrast, he's barely broken a sweat.

His voice is a husky murmur: "I don't think this is how you disarmed Lutz."

I make a frustrated noise at him, trying to get my balance back, but I only succeed in bumping my lower half against his in a very indelicate way. My right knee is already resting against his hip and the movement frees it. My leg ends up hooked around his hips, my hands gripping his shoulders and my lady parts smashed up against his...

I freeze.

If I let go I'll topple over, but this position is sending all the wrong signals through my body. *Holy smokes.* I fight the burning impulse to tip my head back and arch into him. I resume breathing, far too fast, my heartbeat crashing like crazy inside my chest. This … whatever this is … is unlike anything I've felt before.

He makes it worse when he leans in, completely in control, his focus solely on my lips. Despite the slight hitch of his breath, his voice becomes an angry growl, dousing me in cold.

"Do you work for Lady Tirelli?" he demands to know.

My eyes widen. That would explain why he locked the door. Lady Tirelli and her boys are butchers. If he's worried I work for her, then his fear for Parker is real.

Outrage rushes through me. "I would never work for her. The Tirelli brothers killed my father!"

I gulp.

Damn him, that's more information than I intended to give. *Damn* my body right now. *Damn* his hand softly stroking my thigh. He could ask me anything and I would answer truthfully.

He frowns, remaining close to me, although his gaze becomes distant for a second as if he's sifting through information in his mind. "I'm familiar with all of their kills. Your name isn't connected with their victims."

Of course it isn't. He thinks I'm Grace Kennedy.

Now I wish I'd picked up the knife when I could have. I need the cold calm right now. I need the strength. I've been known to break down doors, rip through walls. With a weapon in my hand, I can get out of this room within moments.

But now I'm sure he left the knife on the table as a test.

If I try to reach it, it will prove to him that I am his enemy.

He was angry about the possibility that I was one of Lady Tirelli's people, so that tells me he is not her ally. Since I returned to Boston under my current alias, I've kept my head down and my ear to the ground, but I've stayed away from that life.

I was stupid enough to tell Lutz Logan my name. Word will get out: Archer Ryan is back.

I am a threat to Lady Tirelli's operations.

She will come for me.

Like it or not, I'm a target. And if the vehemence in Cain's voice is any indication, he might be my only ally right now. But the way he's looking at me … like I'm his worst nightmare…

I thump my fist against his chest, surprising him with the frustrated gesture. "Damn it! Why did you have to be nice to me this morning? You should have left me on the curb. Anyone else would have."

He appears speechless for the first time, his

ferocity turning to puzzlement. For a second he sways closer, his lips a breath away from mine. "Who *are* you?"

I can't lie. I squeeze my eyes shut and thump my head against the wall, trying to beat the frustration out of myself. Telling the truth is hard for me, but it turns out that lying to Cain Carter is impossible.

"My real name … is Archer Ryan. I'm Patrick Ryan's daughter. If you know about Lady Tirelli, then I assume you know who my father was."

Shock flashes across Cain's face. His green eyes widen. "Archer Ryan."

He switches gears so rapidly it makes my head spin. He removes his hand from my side, releases my thigh, and smoothly extricates himself from the circle of my leg in one swift movement.

He relocates himself two quick paces away.

I wait for the inevitable "But you're a woman," but it doesn't come. Maybe he's in shock or…

I frown at the cool respect in his gaze. He knows my reputation.

He looks at me differently now and … I hate it.

He gives me a nod filled with the wary regard he would hold for a fellow warrior, a combatant, but not a friend. He stands tall, hands at his sides, fingertips lightly curled into loose fists, clearly reassessing everything he thought he knew about me.

I want to go back to being café Grace, a girl who

carries books in her pockets and chews her fingernails. A girl who is not a threat and just needed a little
help.

Not a woman who could burn down his house.

I smooth down my clothing with a sigh. "So, you
see, I would never work for Lady Tirelli. I would
never associate with her sons who were responsible
for killing my father and turning me into a fugitive."

His voice is deadpan: "It was never confirmed that
the Tirelli brothers killed your father. A friend of mine
tried to find out but she had no luck getting that
information."

"Is that the same friend who doesn't tell you when
she's hurt?"

"Possibly."

I draw my shoulders back. "I want you to know
that I don't have any intention of harming you or your
sister. What happened this morning was a mistake." I
shake my head in frustration. "But I couldn't stand by
and watch Briar die. She's a nice old lady who clearly
doesn't get enough food and she's the closest person I
have to a friend, even though I barely spoke to her, so
that probably tells you a lot about my relationships
with other people."

I try to draw a breath. Information is free-flowing
from my mouth and I have to make it stop. I clench
my hands and focus on the floor. "I won't hurt you or

your family. All I want is to walk out of here and disappear. You won't see me again."

His response is sharp. "I can't let you do that."

I frown, looking up at him again. "Why? Because I'm wanted by the police? Because I'm a violent criminal? Because I've killed my fair share of assholes?"

He closes the gap and his cold demeanor disappears. The depth of emotion in his voice is unsettling. "Because ... I can't let you die."

I attempt to laugh. "I'm not going to die simply by walking out of here. Really, I can take care of myself."

He says, "Believe me, Grace, if you leave my side, you'll be dead by the end of the day."

CHAPTER FOUR

I shiver. He sounds so certain that harm is going to come to me.

He is cautious as he asks, "Did Briar say anything to you?"

I frown. "She told me a lot of things that I have trouble believing."

"Like what?"

"That Lutz Logan is an assassin. That assassins have a code and I broke it by interfering. She told me to go to a bookstore. She said I'd be safe there."

He nods. "The Tomb."

I'm surprised. "That's the one."

His eyes meet mine. "But you don't believe any of it."

I shake my head. "Not remotely. Assassins are a myth."

A smile plays around his mouth. "So is Archer Ryan."

I have no comeback for that. I blow out an exhale, fold my arms across my chest, and focus on my dropped coat. "Even if I believe any of it, you don't owe me anything. Not help, and certainly not protection."

"Hmm."

His murmur is ambiguous. I can't tell if he means "Hmm, you're right" or "Hmm, you're wrong," or maybe "Hmm, there's no hope for you at all."

He says, "There's something I need to show you. I think it will clarify things for you."

He digs into his pocket and pulls out a thick gold band. It looks like a wedding ring. I guess he's full of secrets. A secret sister and now a secret wife. I'm not sure why he wants me to see it, but whatever. It's fine. I study the floor for a moment, trying to squash my unexpected feelings of disappointment and envy. She is a lucky woman.

"Grace?"

I give myself a shake and meet his eyes. "You're married."

He frowns, tilting his head as if he missed something, then his expression clears. "No, but it's important that you understand who I really am."

He lifts his hand so that I have a clear view of the

ring. He slips it onto the forefinger of his left hand, not onto his ring finger.

He says, "I'm about to break a rule, but it's a small transgression and worth it to prove to you what you're up against."

He keeps his hand pressed across his chest so I can't miss the ring. It glints, as if someone opened a window and the sun hit the metal band.

Then...

He glows at the edges, just like Lutz Logan did. I blink rapidly, trying to stay focused on him, but it's like trying to stare at a bright spot. I reach out, but his backlit figure recedes. He steps away and...

He disappears.

Just like that, Cain is gone.

I gasp, my heart suddenly hammering in my chest. I turn in circles, trying to locate him. It's like he stepped into his surroundings, blended into them. It isn't ... possible.

Dad once told me that not everything is as it seems, that there are instruments of magic that humans can use to make themselves stronger and quicker, and that magical beings walk among us. I took his warnings with a grain of salt. Magic is for fairy tales. Fairy tales have no part in my life.

I close my eyes and inhale a calming breath. I know Cain hasn't left the room, because the door hasn't opened. He could be leaning up against it, watching me, or he could be a lot closer…

When I fought Lutz, I had a weapon in my hands, a conduit to the strength and calm that otherwise remains inaccessible to me. I need to be calm now, to open my senses. I reacted by instinct to Lutz, so maybe if I allow myself to react instinctively to Cain…

That's a dangerous thought. My reactions to Cain are like nothing I've experienced before. Allowing myself to focus on them means magnifying them.

I shake off my fears and quiet my thoughts, taking deep, slow breaths. Within moments my heart rate calms. Everything becomes silent and still inside me. I focus on the memory of Cain's hand on my thigh, the way it had both calmed and provoked me.

My senses burn.

Cain.

His presence is like a flame to me, located to my left. I sense a shift in the air, a quiet heartbeat, and … his hand, inches from the side of my face as if he would dare to brush his fingertips across my cheek.

A smile grows on my face despite my best efforts to hide it.

My eyes flash open and my hand snakes out. I latch onto his arm, pull and twist. At the same time, I hook my leg behind his and pull, dragging him off balance so fast he has nowhere to go but the floor. He thuds onto it, rolling slightly to absorb the impact. I follow him down, my hand still clamped around his arm, my left knee crashing onto the hard tiles. *Ouch.*

I ignore the pain, my right leg tangled in his. I'm straddling his hips, pressed low against his chest because he has caught me there, his arms holding me tight. I push one hand against the floor to keep my face above his.

His features are still blurry at the edges, difficult to focus on, but I refuse to look away. He looks stunned, uncertain for the very first time. It's hard to miss his wide eyes or his quick inhale.

Just like Lutz, he asks, "How did you see...?"

I shake my head, answering honestly: "I have no idea." Then I exhale, bursting with my own questions. *"What is this?"*

His edges become rapidly sharp, materializing, fully visible again. He stays very still, making no attempt to remove himself from beneath me.

He says, "I'm an assassin."

I shoot back, "Assassins don't exist."

He arches an eyebrow at me. "Clearly, I do."

He certainly does. All hulking six and a half feet of him. His body is warm beneath mine. I'm acutely aware of the way his muscles move, shifting with every breath he takes. I press my lips together, inches away from his.

I'm not often bewildered, but right now I have no idea how to react. If he's an assassin, then he has killed people, but … so have I. He knows how to fight, but so do I. I can't judge him in any way that doesn't bring judgement back on myself.

"Are you human?" I stare down at him, a portion of my hair sliding loose and falling across my face as I hold my breath for his answer.

"Yes." He tucks my hair behind my ear with the hand on which he wears the ring. "This is an assassin's ring. It gives me power to do … unusual things."

The golden band gives off a faint glow, a warmth that both pulls and pushes at me. It gets worse when he curls his fingers softly at the base of my neck, resting them there.

Before I can ask him anything else, he says, "So this is how you disarmed Lutz Logan."

My cheeks heat up. "Not quite like this. It was more of a roundhouse kick. In fact … he disarmed himself when he stabbed me with his knife."

A confused frown descends over Cain's features. "When he nicked your chin?"

"No … he stabbed my side."

Alarm shoots across Cain's face. He places both hands on my hips, easily lifting me up and away from him, rising up beneath me so fast it makes my head spin. Within seconds, I'm back on my feet and he's bending over me, tugging at the base of my shirt.

His demand is urgent. "Which side? Where are you hurt?"

I'm frozen, gasping as his fingertips brush across the bare skin above my right hip.

Not finding a wound there, he turns to the other side.

I clamp my hand over his, forcing him to look at me while I try to find my voice. "I ... he ... I'm okay. He didn't hurt me. The knife lodged in my book."

He pauses. "The book you were carrying in your pocket?"

I scowl. "That thug stabbed through all the pages."

He nearly smiles. But not quite. "So the book took the death blow."

When I nod, he murmurs, more to himself than to me: "Could that be the end of it? A failed kill?" He shakes his head. "It was all a continuance of the act of interference. *Damn.* They still have the right to come after you."

I can't seem to let go of his hand. None of what he said makes sense to me. "You need to explain what's going on."

He runs his free hand through his hair, straightening, allowing me to keep his other hand pressed against my side. I feel foolish, holding on to his hand like this, but the fact that he disappeared right before my eyes has shaken me. I'm worried he'll disappear again. Everything Briar was trying to warn me about is suddenly a very real possibility.

He says, "Briar told you the truth. Lutz Logan is a

brutal assassin. He's part of the Assassin's Legion. The Master of the Legion is Slade Baines. When you saved Briar's life, you broke a major rule in the Assassin's Code."

I can't breathe. I tell myself it has nothing to do with the warmth of his hand resting against my side or the way his fingertips flex against my too-thin shirt. I also don't want to admit that I'm a little shaken. "What rule?"

"The fifth rule: A bystander who prevents an assassination forfeits their own life."

I stare at him. "Which means?"

"Slade Baines has the right to kill you."

I burst out, "On what planet does that make sense? Any good person could try to stop someone getting killed. You can't kill them for trying to help!"

A dangerous smile lights his eyes. "Anyone can try. But nobody has ever succeeded. Only someone who is a true threat can stop a fully-trained assassin. You kicked Lutz sideways. There aren't many assassins who would dare to take him on, let alone beat him."

I narrow my eyes at Cain. Something tells me he's one of the few who would.

He shakes his head. "What's more, you saw through his blur. I didn't believe it when my people reported that Archer Ryan had resurfaced, stopped Briar's assassination, and defeated Lutz Logan by seeing through his blur…"

"What's a 'blur?'"

He refocuses on me. "It's what assassins call becoming invisible. We blur into our surroundings so we can't be seen. It's very unusual for someone to see through it."

I lick my suddenly dry lips. I've taken on a lot of thugs. Fought a lot of battles. But assassins ... there's a reason they belong in the category of nightmares and demons that live in the shadows. There's a reason I don't want to believe they exist. There were whispers that Dad's protector, the Glass Fox, was an assassin, but I always closed my ears to those stories. I never saw her and I never wanted to. I had enough violence in my life.

Cain's hand flexes against my ribcage. "Slade Baines will come for you whether he wants to or not. You are a threat. He is duty bound to follow the code and end your life. He is also one of the most ruthless assassins in our history. If he finds you..."

Cain's grip tightens and a chill runs down my spine.

I whisper, "You're one of them. I'm not safe with you either."

I can't help glancing at the door. He doesn't miss it. I'm pretty sure he doesn't miss the desperation growing on my face either. I may have put him on the floor momentarily, but he's already proved how easily he can beat me in a fight. This man is like no one I've ever fought. And that was before he put that damn ring on.

He draws himself up to his full height, repositioning his hand against my side, but he doesn't remove it from beneath mine. Instead, he moves closer. Despite my growing fear, I grip his hand more tightly. I tell myself it's because I'm keeping him in that position so I can pull him off balance if I need to, not because I need the human connection right now. The foundations of my world have shifted and Cain's touch is the pressure point keeping me focused.

His voice is quiet, unthreatening: "Grace, you have nothing to fear from me. I'm not part of Slade's Legion. I belong to a Faction called the Horde, which is based in the South. I was given permission to stay in Boston so I could see my sister. Unfortunately, the situation with Lady Tirelli has become very dangerous and I need to take Parker south where she will be safe. I want you..."

He pauses, inhaling, exhaling, as if he's choosing his words with care. "I want you to come with me, too."

I consider him warily. I'm not sure if I heard him correctly. "If Slade Baines is as fierce as you say he is, then I'm not safe anywhere."

A smile curves the corner of Cain's mouth. "He isn't allowed to follow us into Horde territory. I can keep you safe there."

I search his eyes for any trace of deceit, any hint of deception or manipulation. I teeter on the edge of believing him.

He leans in closer than I would normally allow anyone to stand to me without retaliating.

His voice lowers. "Come with me, Grace."

I suddenly realize that despite knowing my real name, he keeps calling me "Grace."

I whisper, "If I ask you to let me walk out of this room right now and allow me to leave this house, will you let me go?"

A muscle in his jaw clenches. But he only hesitates for a moment.

He slides his hand out from under mine, prowls to the door, and curls his hand around the handle. The lock clicks at his touch. He swings it wide and leans against the doorframe, but not in a position that blocks the opening. He also removes his assassin's ring, placing it back into his pocket.

He says, "I hope you won't go."

I rub my waist where his warmth is now absent, chewing my lip in thought. I retrieve my coat from the floor, my shoulder bag from the countertop, and keep both close to my chest as I proceed quietly past him.

He holds his breath.

I pause long enough to ask, "Does Parker know about any of this?"

He shakes his head. "Not yet. But the time is fast approaching when I'll have to tell her."

"And Sarah?"

"She knows."

I don't hesitate. I've already made my choice.

I step through the door. His forehead creases in a worried frown. He takes a small step toward me but stops himself, his arms tight at his sides.

He follows me while I make my way through the maze of his home. I sense his every breath, every twitch of his muscles. I know every moment that he reaches for me but stops himself. By the time I return to the entrance where Parker left us, his frustration with the situation is showing in all his tense edges.

He believes that if I leave this house, I'll die.

But he also made it clear that he won't make me stay. I've never met a man with this much self-control. Never a man who had this much respect for my right to decide my own fate.

I pause in the entrance room, a little bit amazed. I consider the front door and then Cain. He might force himself to let me leave, but he hasn't taken his stormy eyes off me.

I keep my tone even: "If I come with you... I will need my things brought too. I don't own much, but I can't afford to replace anything. Especially my books."

He lets out his held breath. He doesn't miss a beat.

"Give me your address, your key, and I'll have everything waiting for you when we arrive in Austin."

"Thank you." I exhale very carefully, shocked by my choice.

I may have made the worst decision of my life.

CHAPTER FIVE

I need that hot chocolate Parker promised me. I wasn't lying when I told them I have low blood pressure. I run cold, with bad circulation, and right now I need sugar. Pronto.

Before I can take a step in the direction of the lounge, the front door opens.

Spencer, Cain's driver, pushes the door open and nods respectfully to Cain. "Someone to see you, sir."

Spencer steps aside to reveal a man dressed in jeans and a t-shirt that accentuate all his muscles. The breath stops in my lungs. I would recognize his amber eyes anywhere. It turns out that he has a shock of light brown hair to go with those eyes. Along with two days of growth that shadows his jaw. He looks like he threw on his clothes without caring about them, but he still manages to look dangerous.

Cain stiffens beside me. He draws himself upright. "What are you doing here, Lutz?"

Unlike the blond guy on the street earlier, Cain's glare isn't sufficient to make Lutz Logan back down. He pauses for the driver to disappear down the front steps before he steps inside and closes the door behind him.

The fact that he invited himself into Cain's home speaks volumes. Cain said he was given permission to stay in Boston. I wonder if that means Slade's Legion can push Cain around as much as they like.

Either that or Lutz has a death wish.

I quickly consider both men. The way Cain's expression darkens makes me think Lutz might be the one breaking the rules right now.

The sound of the door closing thuds in my ears and echoes around the suddenly charged space. The growing threat and aggression in Cain's expression is a shock to me. When he fought me, he was cool and in control. Now, he angles his body slightly forward, releasing one clenched fist to curve gently around my left shoulder. He's preparing to place himself between us if he has to.

I brace for Lutz to recognize me, waiting to find out whether my identity as Archer Ryan—the very *male* Archer Ryan—is still intact.

Lutz gives me a cursory glance before he dismisses

me. All he sees is a woman. He's looking for Archer, not Grace.

I resume breathing.

Lutz's response is a forceful statement. "You know why I'm here."

Cain growls back, "You'll have to elaborate."

If I were Lutz, I would run for the hills right now, but I guess Cain was right about Lutz's ferocity. He meets Cain's hard stare while taking up position several paces away, feet planted, shoulders squared. I recognize the fighting stance. It reminds me to relax my own body language. I've instinctively shifted my weight ready for an attack, but remaining in that position will only draw Lutz's attention. My best defense right now is to blend in, pretend to be the woman that I appear to be.

Lutz's response to Cain's aggression is to narrow his eyes and flex his fists. I change my mind about the idea that the Legion is allowed to push Cain around. Lutz clearly has a death wish.

He asks, "Where is Archer Ryan?"

Cain snaps, "If the Legion wants information from me, then Slade can do me the respect of asking me himself."

A muscle ticks in Lutz's jaw, but for the first time his expression becomes disquieted, revealing more than hard lines and determination.

He says, "Slade is dealing with something else right now. Locating Archer is up to me."

Cain considers Lutz's response. Whatever the "something else" might be, it seems to give him pause. He changes tack, replying smoothly, "Archer Ryan is long gone. He bumped into me on the street but I let him go. I won't interfere in your operations."

Lutz suddenly focuses on me, his cool gaze dragging up and down me for a moment before he inclines his head at the stitches on my chin. "That looks nasty, sweetheart."

I can't risk speaking; he might recognize my voice. It's bad enough that I'm clutching my coat in my arms that I was wearing when I fought him, but at least it's rolled up. I lower my gaze to the floor as if I'm intimidated. It kills me, but it's the best way to hide my eyes in case he recognizes them.

The silence stretches out a moment too long and my heart rate speeds up.

Cain shifts beside me, a new edge of tension entering his voice. "I've told you everything I know. It's time for you to go—"

"Cain?" Parker appears in the doorway to the expansive lounge, a steaming mug cradled in her hands. She has let down her hair and changed into skinny jeans and a soft sweater that hugs her curves. Her feet are bare, colorful toenails a sharp contrast to the white marble floor. She is tall, graceful, and looks like she could have stepped out of a magazine.

Unlike the rest of us, she is completely relaxed.

Her gaze lands on Lutz. "Oh. Hi."

She gives him a smile that lights up her eyes in a way that would melt the hardest heart.

He was clearly not expecting it.

He freezes. Then he glances at Cain.

If Lutz is remotely observant, he'll identify the family resemblance as quickly as I did.

When he turns back to Parker, all of the aggression drains out of him in a rush, as if she shattered it with her shy smile.

His line of sight doesn't leave her face. He seems transfixed by her stunning eyes. His singular focus is a far cry from the offensive full-body once-over he gave me. In fact, he looks like someone just hit him over the head.

He manages a rough, "Hi." Then he quickly frowns at himself. "Uh…"

A curious frown settles on Parker's forehead. She is either oblivious to the testosterone in the room or she's choosing to ignore it.

Hmm. I hide a smile as I quickly assess her carefully casual demeanor. She's not stupid. I wonder how much of our conversation she heard before she decided to make a timely appearance to defuse the escalating situation.

She turns to Cain: "I just made Grace a hot chocolate. Should I make one for your friend?"

Cain's response is firm. "No, thank you, Parker. Lutz won't be staying."

"Oh, okay." Parker side-eyes Lutz as she speaks, a hint of caution appearing on her features.

What I know of Parker so far is that she's quiet and kind-hearted. She might have thought she could intervene, but she obviously didn't sneak a look at Lutz before she stepped into the doorway. There's not much that could prepare a woman for all the grisly ferocity that is Lutz Logan, especially with that shadowy beard he has going on that makes him look like he needs someone to take care of him.

I have to admire how effortlessly she has floored him. It actually makes me a little envious. I never learned how to be feminine. By necessity, my behavior around men leans toward avoidance or defensive aggression.

Now that Lutz has lost his threatening stance, I'm a little bit thrown myself. He looks … lost. Like hatred is his fuel and now that it's gone, he's not sure where to turn.

He gives Parker a gruff but polite nod. "Thank you for the offer. I'll be going now."

He swings to Cain and his expression darkens again. Lutz's anger is back. He says, "Don't forget why it was me today and not you."

He steps toward the door without taking his eyes off Cain. Then he pushes it wide and strides through it, powerful strides carrying him away as the door closes behind him, leaving cold air in his wake.

Cain is quiet beside me. He stares at the door, unmoving. Whatever Lutz meant by his final comment, it seems to have hit Cain hard.

My attention is drawn to Parker when she shivers. Her bare feet might not be a problem in front of the fireplace, but it's cold in here.

She looks a little pale. "Who was that guy? I've never seen anyone like him." She laughs, but it's forced. "Well, other than my brother."

I swivel and take her arm, careful not to upset the liquid in the mug she's clinging to. With another glance at Cain, who is still in deep thought, I draw her into the lounge room. "It's really nice of you to make that for me."

She gives me a small smile. "I figure you mostly make food for other people, so you deserve some T.L.C. for a change."

She hands me the mug as we reach the fireplace. I'm conscious that Cain hasn't followed us yet and a small level of worry invades my stomach. My initial impression was that Lutz and Cain were enemies, but experience has shown me that relationships are complicated. There's more going on here than I know about, and somehow Briar, Lutz, and Cain are all tied up in it.

It's surprising to me that Parker is so accepting of my presence. Of course ... I might not be the first woman Cain has brought home at a moment's notice.

Regardless, she hasn't questioned me and I'm grateful. I don't want her trust to be misplaced.

I hug the hot chocolate as I sink into the nearest chair. "So ... uh ... I got into some trouble this morning and Cain is helping me out. That guy who was here ... he's mixed up in it too." I run my hand over my chin. The anesthetic is wearing off and my stitches sting a little. "Sorry, I know that doesn't really explain anything."

Parker picks up her own cup and curls her feet under her bottom on the couch. She stares into her cup for a moment before she says, "Cain is super protective of me. He didn't know about me until Dad died. I didn't know about Cain either. You can imagine how fun it was at the reading of Dad's will."

She gives a short laugh. "This giant guy walks in and I'm like ... who is this person? And why the hell has he paid off Dad's debts?"

She levels her gaze with me. "My point is ... don't believe what you read about my brother in those magazines. Cain never brings people here. Ever. But he brought you. If he trusts you, then so do I. No questions asked."

I swallow the chocolate and it warms my insides. Despite my tough act, I'm not a winter person. But it's not only the drink that has warmed me. I'm pretty sure Parker is the first person who has ever placed their trust in me without question. Even Dad looked at me as if I was going to stab him in the back.

Cain interrupts my thoughts, appearing at my side, but he speaks to Parker. "There's been a change of plans. We need to leave right away."

Her eyes widen. "Right now?"

He settles onto the seat beside her. "I know it's sudden, but..." He produces his phone, turning the screen toward her.

Her face falls. "Oh. The reporters know about me."

Cain hands me the phone. The newsfeed shows an image of him and Parker outside the café.

She looks up at him as I hand back the phone.

She asks, "Will it be any different in Austin?"

He grins. "I'm old news there. And the tabloids here will find something else to write about once I'm gone." He hugs her. "I promise, this is a good change."

She sighs. "You're right. There are too many memories here. It's time to make new ones."

He smiles at her, brushing the hair out of her eyes. "Bring whatever you've packed already. I'll have everything else packed and brought to us."

His smile broadens. "I'm bringing Grace's things, too."

Parker's lips part in surprise. "Grace is coming with us?"

"She is."

Parker considers me for a moment. Then she smiles at her brother. She gives him a look I can't decipher. It makes him arch an eyebrow at her.

She says, "Okay. Good."

"Good?" he asks.

She grins. "Good."

I look between them, not sure what their silent communication means, but Parker takes my hand and rushes me upstairs to find spare clothing that will fit me while I'm waiting for my things to arrive in Austin. The next ten minutes are a whirlwind of activity. Cain disappears to get changed, emerging in a white collared shirt that is open at the neck, gray pants tailored to fit his frame. Staff race around the house and Cain talks nonstop on his phone, organizing everything from a private jet to our transport when we get there.

I'm tuned in to the changes in his voice now. I can tell the difference between his conversations with civilians and when he's speaking to his "people."

I don't know exactly who those people are, but something tells me it won't be long before I find out.

CHAPTER SIX

*W*e touch down at the airport, where several vehicles wait at the airport to take us to our destination. Cain explained during the flight that he has a small place in the city where we can stay for a while, but he wants Parker to choose their new home once she decides which college she wants to attend. Dr. Mathers and Cain's regular driver, Spencer, came with us, along with a small number of his staff.

The vehicle I travel in with Cain and Parker is roomy, with seats facing each other so we can all sit in the back. Sarah takes the other car, telling us she'll see us there. As I find my seat, my bag clutched in my lap containing the only worldly possessions I brought with me, my reckless decision hits me.

Cain asked me to come with him. He said he could

keep me safe in Horde territory, but I don't really know what that means. I replay the conversations he had with Parker on the plane—none of it involved an explanation about where I'm supposed to stay or with whom.

The flight here was a fairy tale, a hiatus from reality, but my guard is back up by the time the vehicle pulls out of the parking lot. All I know for sure is that I got a free ride out of Boston and Cain has promised to transport my things. I have no guarantees beyond that, and every time I try to ask, my throat clams up.

Why did I make myself vulnerable like this?

It makes me ache to realize that a small piece of kindness only leaves me wanting more. I tell myself to get it together. He's not going to ditch me right away or leave me on the street. I'll take whatever accommodation he offers me tonight and then I'll find my own place. It's nothing I haven't done a thousand times before.

I sense Cain's gaze on me as I stare resolutely out of the window, the cityscape passing by as I calm my nerves by memorizing street names. It gives me something to focus on and helps me reconnect with my tough side. Within minutes, I'm calm and in control again.

Then Cain's phone rings into the silence.

He gives the screen a curious frown before he answers. Whatever the other person says, Cain's first reaction is surprise. Then it quickly disappears as another short and cryptic conversation ensues.

Unlike his earlier conversations with his people, this one causes an edge of tension to tighten his mouth and crease his forehead. At one point, I'm sure he looks at me. My senses prickle, but when I raise my eyes, his gaze is fixed on the window. He hangs up and peers out at the passing streets for a long minute before he tells the driver to change direction.

Parker leans forward. "Cain?"

He turns back to her with a reassuring smile. "We need to take a detour to a … military facility that I own. It's a training camp of sorts for civilian contractors. There's a problem I have to sort out that can't wait."

His gaze lands on me and I don't know how to decipher his thoughts. There are so many lies in what he said that my ears buzz. Parker might buy the story about a military facility, but I don't. Knowing what I do about Cain, I'm immediately thinking assassins. Maybe a base of operations. Now, there's a delightful thought.

Cain is tight-lipped after that, so I guess I'll have to wait and see if my theory pans out.

We head into downtown Austin, travel through a maze of streets, and turn off into a parking garage signed as Capital Visitors Parking. I'm not familiar with Austin, but I think we're close to the Texas Capitol.

We exit the vehicle into the parking garage and I'm momentarily disoriented when Cain leads us to a door on the far side marked "Authorized Personnel Only."

Cain casually pulls Parker into his side as he takes hold of the handle, keeping her close. His free hand darts out at the last moment and catches my arm.

The door swings inward.

We step into an open courtyard and he releases me.

Our surroundings make me frown. It's odd that the door led us straight outside. On either side of us, official-looking buildings squat at the side of a wide, pebbled entranceway. The courtyard ahead of us is expansive enough to host a large gathering. A high stone fence curves out from the door behind and around the entire space. Farther in the distance, a beautiful cathedral soars into the sky, a gorgeous contrast to the drab buildings located close by.

Men and women jog in military rows, weaving in and out of the buildings, and disappear toward the perimeter. They're all wearing typical khaki green shirts and long pants. It certainly looks like a military camp, but I'm not convinced.

I sense Cain's gaze on me, but when I turn, his focus is fixed on the cathedral. He points. "I need to go to that building there. Come with me, please."

Parker and I follow him. The closer we get to the

cathedral, the more on edge Cain becomes, his shoulders tense, and his responses to Parker's questions shorter than normal.

I notice with curiosity that he leads us along the meandering pathway in such a way that the weaving joggers never encounter us. My senses buzz the nearer we get to the cathedral. This whole place feels off, but this particular building...

A dangerous friction fills the air that makes the hairs on my arms stand on end. A giant sandstone arch provides shade at the front, but the cold feels too cold.

I shiver despite myself as Cain draws us beneath the arch.

Once again, his gaze darts to me as if he's trying to figure something out just by looking at me. That's the third time he's done that and it's unsettling to say the least.

He says, "I want you both to stay right here for now. This building houses a lot of weapons, so it's protected by some very dangerous security mechanisms. Don't try to follow me inside. I'm not exaggerating when I say that you could be killed. I promise I won't be long. Maybe five minutes. Can I trust you to stay right here?"

His gaze bores into me, the edge of anxiety in his expression heightening my own.

I give him a very definite nod. There's nothing I

want to do less than venture further inside this building. "Parker and I will stay here."

"Absolutely, big brother." Parker smiles despite the brevity of Cain's warning. "I have no plans to get dead today. I had enough excitement meeting that guy this morning. I'm happy to stay out of trouble."

"Good." He relaxes a little. Seeming satisfied that we will follow his instructions, he disappears into the dark recesses of the entranceway and beyond, his footsteps receding.

Parker leans against the side of the building, her dark hair spreading against the sandstone while I shift my weight impatiently, examining our surroundings for threats. If the people who live here are assassins, then I don't want to meet them.

Parker's hand darts out to snag my arm, but her touch is gentle. "You're making me nervous, Grace. What's wrong?"

I can't tell her that we're surrounded by assassins right now. And I sure as anything can't describe how much I *don't* like this building we're sheltering against. There's no way to explain the extent to which my senses are firing alarms at me. But, above all, my uncertainty about what's going to happen after today bubbles to the surface.

I stop pacing and bite my lip. I can't stop myself tapping my thigh. My anxiety has to go somewhere. "I've never done anything like this. Gone to a strange place with people I've only known for a few hours. I ... honestly..."

My shoulders sag. Finger stops tapping. "Cain doesn't owe me more than he's already given me. In fact, he doesn't owe me anything at all. I don't want to overstay my welcome."

Her gaze softens. She lifts herself off the wall. "I want to tell you something, but not because I'm looking for sympathy. I think it might help you understand what kind of man Cain is." She bites her own lip in a way that tells me she's about to open her heart.

She says, "Dad was agoraphobic. Do you know what that means?"

"He feared the outside world?"

"Basically, yes. It started after Mom died. At which time he also became very protective of me. To the point where ... I was overprotected. I didn't go out. Didn't go to parties. He let me go to school, but that was all.

"When Cain came into my life, he changed everything. He got me into college, walked me to class when I needed him to, encouraged me to go on my own as soon as I was ready. He took me jogging every morning. At first it was just around the yard. Then around the city. The trip to the café this morning was supposed to be another step to get me back out there, you know."

She takes both my hands. "You see ... once Cain

commits to something, he doesn't back out. He's all in. He asked you to come with us, and even though I don't know what sort of trouble you're in, I know he wants you to stay with us for as long as you want to be here." A genuine smile graces her lips. "And you know what? So do I."

I chew my lip. She has been so open with me. Kinder than anyone I've ever met in my life. I want to show her the same honesty, but I don't know how to share the details of my screwed-up life. I also don't know how to ask her why she wants me around. Anyone who ever helped me wanted something in return. I can't figure out what Cain and Parker gain from my presence.

For now, I'm willing to take her statement at face value. My voice is small, no match for the warmth of emotion I feel right now. "Thank you."

She releases my hands and tilts her head side to side. "I really need to stretch right now. Going straight from the plane to the car did not do me any favors. Do you think Cain's mandate extends to the turf right there?"

She points at a patch of grass just outside the archway.

I purse my lips. "Cain was very specific…"

She contemplates the sky for a moment before she strolls outward into the sunlight. "He was, but it can't hurt to take two steps this way, right? See, two steps.

That's all."

I put down my bag and try to relax, too. I can't help but smile at Parker. If she lived her life isolated like she said she did, then taking steps like this are acts of courage for her. I can't squash that.

Her smile broadens as she holds her arms out for me to join her. For a moment, I glimpse the same carefree spirit I witnessed at the café this morning—a young woman who hasn't lost her belief in good despite all the bad in the world.

She tips her head back, closes her eyes, and looks like she's soaking up the sun for all it's worth. It's much warmer here, and I have to admit, I'm loving the fact that I'm thawing out after Boston's cold.

I remain in the shadows where I belong.

Pounding footsteps draw my attention left.

The procession of running warriors charges around the corner, their current pace faster than their previous gentle jog. Their leader runs backward as she shouts orders at them. She doesn't see Parker and she's moments away from colliding with her.

I jump forward. "Parker, watch out!"

Parker twists. Her eyes fly open. She tries to get out of the way, but the woman crashes into her, knocking Parker flying.

Parker ends up on her bottom in the grass, just outside the paved cathedral entranceway, wincing as she thuds against the ground. She's lucky she didn't land on the stone pavement.

The woman teeters off course, wobbling violently in the opposite direction, but manages to stay upright. She comes to a halt several paces away, her face red, her sharp gaze landing on Parker—the culprit who knocked into her.

The soldiers pull up sharp when she screams at them, "Halt!"

I rush to Parker's side, holding my hand out to her. Before I can help her stand, the woman crosses the distance, shouting at us as she moves: "What sort of clumsy losers are they sending me now?"

My gaze narrows. *What...?*

She is dressed like the others in a khaki shirt and pants, but she carries a baton at her waist, clipped to her belt. I'm shocked when she unclips it, raises it above her head, and prepares to swing it at Parker in one brutal movement.

Parker freezes on the ground, eyes wide, her face pale, a cry of fear on her lips. She isn't trained like me to run or fight. She's still learning to cope with the outside world. The coming violence must be nothing short of terrifying for her. She curls up, throwing her arms over her face to protect herself.

I dart between them, hunch and twist, taking the blow across my left shoulder.

Thwack.

Pain explodes through my upper arm, searing every nerve in my back.

Oh, hell, that thing is made of metal, not wood.

I roar out the pain, expelling it by focusing on the sound screaming out of my lungs, pressing my fingernails into my thighs. Stronger than pain, anger courses through me.

The baton would have cracked Parker's cheekbone.

This woman hasn't stopped to ask us who we are or why we're here. She simply retaliated with violence. What kind of person is she? There's no reason for her behavior. Other than sheer dumb arrogance.

But the answer is in what Cain revealed to me: this woman is an assassin. They all are. Violence is in their nature.

Well, I'm not afraid of them.

Parker's wide eyes meet mine. "Grace!"

I don't have time to reassure her that I'm okay. My pain-filled roar turns into a shout as I round on the woman: "Get the hell away from my friend!"

The woman's hard features swing into view. She looks even more furious than before, adjusting her grip on the weapon, her knuckles turning white around it. She's ready to swing it again. This time at me. "You will not speak to me like that, Novice!"

I don't know what a "Novice" is. The way she says it, it sounds like some sort of insult. I don't care right now. All I care about is protecting Parker.

I hear Parker scuffle backward, a sensible move that gives me room to defend her. I wish I could reassure her that I won't let anything happen to her, but I need to keep my full attention on this woman and the asshole assassins who are all glaring at me.

I grit my teeth and splay my arms wide, turning myself into a shield. "You don't want this fight. Walk away. Right now."

Aggression pops from every angle of her face and the offensive position she's taking. Instead of backing off, she raises the baton in a swift movement, this time aiming it for my face.

I grab the weapon mid-air, my fist closing around it so fast that she gasps, blinking at me in shock. I hold it tight, my hand clamped around hers. She struggles against me, but the harder she tries to break free, the firmer my grip becomes.

I've grabbed it with my left hand—the arm she hurt. Despite the pain shooting through my shoulder, a smile lifts the corners of my lips.

I'm holding a weapon.

Now the calm seeps through every part of my body, my arms, legs, heart, and mind. My vision becomes sharp, clear, and controlled.

Cain hasn't reappeared, and even if he does, there's no guarantee that he has any control over this woman.

It's down to me for now.

The other assassins form a line that extends from

one side of the cathedral, arcing around us to the other side. They completely block any escape in that direction, and there's no way I'm running into the cathedral.

Meanwhile, the woman continues to push against me, but I'm in control of the baton now. It will take a mere twist to disarm her.

My voice is dangerously soft. "Back off or I will kill you."

"How dare you threaten me, *Novice!*" she hisses.

Yep. Novice is definitely an insult.

I grin. "I thought so."

Her left fist flies at me, but I see it coming a mile away. I block the strike, my right arm thumping against hers, intercepting her attack. That's when I retaliate, my knee connecting with her stomach, forcing her to flex forward. At the same time, I shove the baton backward so that her fingers open.

I lift the weapon right out of her hand.

Flipping the baton into my right hand, I spin past her and whack it against her shoulder, forcing her to the side. I hit her in the same spot that she hit me. She drops with a cry, grabbing at her arm.

Huh. I didn't hit her that hard. Nowhere near as hard as she hit me. I'm going to have a whopping bruise later, but for now the calm will keep me pain-free.

I adjust my balance and my grip on the weapon as she twists to face me, drawing herself upright, her angry eyes meeting mine. Her glare tells me she isn't going to let this go.

But at least she's forgotten Parker.

I have her full attention.

One of the soldiers in the line behind her shouts, "Let us know when you want help, Brenna."

She smirks back at him. "She's nothing I can't handle."

I turn the baton over in my hand, testing its weight and balance. *Sure thing, honey.*

She launches at me, one fist flying at my face, the other at my stomach. I block the first and evade the second. When she tries to grab my right arm in an attempt to retrieve the baton, I swing my left, thumping her squarely on the cheek. She rockets backward, but lashes out when I follow. She lets fly with strike after strike but I block each and follow up with a clip to her head, again with my left hand, which doesn't have the power of my right. This time when she swivels back to me, I spin and kick, my foot connecting squarely with her torso.

She flies sideways into the grass, ducking and rolling at the last moment, shaking herself as she jumps to her feet. For a second, I think she's going to stop, but she barges right back at me.

I'm tired of giving her second chances.

I swap the baton to my left hand and go on the attack, my right fist a blur as I jab at her face, shoulder, and uppercut her jaw, all while using my left arm and the baton to block her attempts to attack, finally sweeping her legs out from under her.

She lands on her butt on the turf.

I tower over her. *"Stay down."*

She tests her jaw, her face red, raw hatred blooming in her eyes. She definitely wasn't expecting me to know how to defend myself.

She yells at the men standing to her right, "Get her!"

I brace for impact, swiftly assessing the potential onslaught.

It takes me all of a second to realize that Brenna isn't talking about me.

She means Parker.

Oh, hell no.

I race after the three guys headed for my friend, clip the first across the shoulder with the baton, grab the second and pull him backward, and thump the third full in the face. They duck and roll, and three more men take their place, launching themselves at me in what looks like a practiced maneuver. A crowd attack.

I block the first with a kick to his face, but the second guy—the biggest yet—gets hold of my arm in a solid wrestling grip, forcing me downward. Two more men pounce as soon as I drop, one pinning my other arm and the other kneeing me in the back.

They keep me down long enough for Brenna to cross the distance, bend, and land a solid hit to my chin. Right on my stitches.

It's a low blow, a dirty tactic. The cut opens up and the pain makes me angry. Oddly enough, it's not because it hurts. It's because Cain went to a lot of trouble over that wound this morning.

So far, I've kept the attackers away from Parker, and if I can achieve that, then it doesn't matter how much I get hurt. I've suffered worse.

But what really chills me is that all of this is a practiced maneuver. A four against one tactic, as if they are trained to gang up on others. Those are mob tactics, the kind I experienced when I was younger. These assholes aren't expecting me to know how to deal with them. What's more, the idiot holding my arm hasn't tried to take the baton away from me.

My right foot shoots backward, knocking into the shin of the guy behind me. Because he has one leg propped on my back, he loses his balance as soon as I hit his standing leg. I continue my sweep, dropping the guy holding one of my arms. From there, it's easy to dislodge the remaining man.

I jump to my feet.

I'm done being cautious.

It's time to use the baton and to hell with the damage.

CHAPTER SEVEN

I thump the weapon against the chest of one of the guys who held me down, spin and kick the other guy, stomp my foot down on the third before he can get up, and then whirl back to land another solid kick to Brenna's chest, propelling her all the way back into the others. Two more kicks, a stomp, and a full fist ensure that all of the men who attacked me are down for the count.

As they groan on the grass around me, I assess the rest of them, my chest heaving. There are at least ten more men and women itching to attack me. I can tell from the way their hands twitch and their feet shift, weight forward, ready to run into the fight as soon as Brenna orders them to.

I'll fight them all if I have to.

The next woman I hit lands close to Parker's location.

Parker has curled up against the side of the building, pressing against it. I have the chance to look at her for the first time since the attack started. She's in shock, curled over her knees, her soft sobs reaching my ears. The sound wrenches my heart around. She doesn't deserve to be exposed to this violence.

But I have no idea how to make it stop. Every time I knock them out, they recover. Short of killing them —which I could do, easily—I'm not sure what to do.

They won't stop.

I want to scream at them. This is a game to them— a game of dominance. But it's real life to me, and it's a nightmare for Parker.

All she wanted was some sun on her face.

The cut on my chin has well and truly opened up. When I swipe at it, my hand comes away coated in blood.

I'm a mess.

But I'm an angry mess.

As I wait for the next attack, ready for it, running footsteps thud behind me.

Cain.

I'm not sure how I know it's him just from listening to his footfalls. He is quick, agile. He steps lightly. His presence is like a force. Maybe it's the assassin's ring and the strange magic in it. Or maybe it's purely him. Either way, my heart lifts. I tell myself it's relief. At least there will be two of us now.

My back is turned toward him, but the assassins are facing in his direction.

One of them shouts, "It's Cain!"

Murmurs ripple through the rest of them. "Cain is back."

The assassins in the background stand to attention and the ones on the ground pull themselves upright, glaring at me as if I'm a bug they want to squash. The way they look at Parker makes my blood boil. It's as if her vulnerability is disgusting to them. But what disturbs me most is the way they look between Cain and me.

They're gloating. It's like they think I'm in deep trouble.

Brenna hisses at me before she steps back. "You're fucked now, Novice."

Cain's footsteps halt abruptly.

I don't want to take my eyes off the assassins, but I need to see what he's doing. I risk a glance backward.

He has frozen in the archway, his focus on Parker. His eyes fly wide, then quickly narrow, his response rapidly hidden behind an expression that resembles granite.

Parker's head is tucked down. She doesn't see him. She's shaking in a way that tears me into pieces. I never wanted her to be exposed to a fight like this.

Ever. And now I can't help her. She's in shock, but all I know is fists and violence.

When Cain steps quietly toward her, she flinches, making him freeze all over again.

He moves away from her position and turns to me.

I try to cover the blood on my chin but it's too late.

He takes in the sight around him: the gloating assassins, my ruined stitches, and the baton in my hand. Last of all Brenna, who smirks at me.

Cain's gaze meets mine and...

Damn. His furious eyes tell me he's mad at me. Seriously mad. He probably thinks I started it, provoked them somehow. After all, I am Archer Ryan. It doesn't matter how many times he calls me "Grace," he can't erase who I really am.

His gaze shifts from me to Brenna. His voice is calm, dangerously controlled. "Brenna? Explain."

She points at Parker. "That Novice bumped into me, so I taught her a lesson."

"How?"

She inclines her head at me. "With the baton."

Cain's expression doesn't change. He doesn't move. "With a weapon you no longer control?"

She frowns. "Well, I did at the time."

He inclines his head at Parker. "You hit this woman with it?"

Brenna shoots back, "I tried to."

"What stopped you?"

Brenna's accusing finger swivels to me. "That one got in the way."

Cain's next question is softer still: "Did you ask them who they are?"

Brenna falters for the first time, glancing between us, but she pushes on. "They're trainees. They need to learn the hard way—"

Cain's deep roar makes the assassins flinch. "*They are not trainees!*"

He strides toward Brenna, his ring glowing, power visible like streams of electricity around his body. His voice lowers to a dangerous snarl. "The woman you tried to assault is my sister."

The blood drains from Brenna's face. She backpedals so fast that she bumps into the men behind her. They don't help her. In fact, they close up so she has nowhere to go.

Cain stops short of touching her. I have no doubt that if she were a man, he would have punched her lights out. It's a double standard, that's for sure. I'd have no trouble doing it for him.

She stammers, "I'm sorry, Master. I didn't know."

Master? I narrow my eyes between them. Cain said Slade was the Master of the Legion, which makes Slade incredibly dangerous. If Cain is the Master of the Horde ... well ... that would explain a few things, like how he fights like a panther and why he only had to glare at an assassin this morning to make him back off.

Cain isn't finished. "The woman who put you on your ass is Grace. She is not a Novice, either. In fact ... Grace is my woman. And she had every right to defend my sister from your unwarranted attack. Be grateful that she did, because if you had harmed Parker, you would not see sunlight for a very long time."

Cain's declaration echoes in my ears. *His woman?*

I try not to appear surprised. I fixate resolutely on a spot on the turf, completely thrown by Cain's description of me. I'm nobody to Cain. I met him this morning. He must simply be using the best label to get everyone to back off.

Cain twists a little, turned in my direction, demanding my attention, a dangerous smile on his lips as he looks at me. The way his gaze travels from my eyes to my toes sends shivers down my spine.

When the silence stretches, Brenna curses. I guess this didn't go the way she wanted. Each of the men who hit me hustles away from her as if they don't want to be anywhere near her—or me for that matter. As if they could hide the fact that they were the ones who came after Parker and me.

Cain pins each of them with his piercing gaze. "You will all report to me after dinner for my verdict."

Heads down, they murmur, "Yes, Master."

Cain narrows his eyes at them, his tone unforgiving. "What?"

They stand to attention. "Yes, Master!"

"Dismissed."

As the gathering clears, Cain makes it clear he's done with all of them. He stops beside me long enough to murmur, "Help me with Parker, please. I've disabled the security mechanisms around the Cathedral. We need to get her inside."

Parker's defensive reflexes kick in and she struggles when he tries to pick her up. I shush her gently as Cain's assassin's ring glows; seconds later she slumps against the wall. He catches her before her head slides to the ground.

Alarm spreads through me. "What did you do to her?"

"I've created an illusion inside her mind. A peaceful one. It will calm her, soothe her fears, and help her recover."

He scoops Parker up into his arms, carrying her inside the building while I follow. I brace for the danger I felt before when I stood close to this building, but it's gone now, making me wonder what kind of security mechanisms he disabled.

So far Cain hasn't said anything about the state of my chin, but I'm sure he'll tackle that problem as soon as he knows Parker is okay.

I'm still holding the baton. I can't let go of it until

I'm sure I can collapse safely. The usual adrenaline drop is seeping in regardless. It's like this place is magnifying the effects. What's more, my back is sore. A dull burn grows in my shoulder blades that I've never felt before and can't seem to shake. I squeeze my eyes closed and open again, putting all my energy into staying focused. I stumble a little but cover it by pretending to examine our surroundings.

Paintings cover the walls—all originals. In some of them, titans battle each other. In others, winged women tear each other apart on the battlefield, their wings glistening and metallic. We climb the stairs to the highest level and my senses buzz all over again as Cain leads me down a corridor to the only doorway.

We enter a large room with an expansive lounge and a small kitchen at the side. It's like a whole apartment in here. A hallway on the right gives me a glimpse of a smaller bedroom and a study. A door on the far left leads to a larger bedroom with an enormous bed.

Cain heads straight to the couch that rests against the far wall, gently laying Parker on it and covering her with a blanket, tucking it around her. He presses his left hand to her forehead for a moment, and when he stands up her chest rises and falls evenly.

He strides to the kitchen area, pulls out a dish towel and raids the fridge, talking as he prepares an icepack. "Parker will sleep now. I can't erase what she saw or the fear she felt, but when she wakes, the memory will be dull and easily forgotten."

There are a thousand memories I'd like to forget. I wish he could do that for me, too. But right now, my anger is stronger than any whimsical wish to erase my past.

"Who were those people?"

He hands me the pack of ice, which I place against my chin with my free hand. He is too perceptive to miss the fact that I haven't put the weapon away.

He says, "I think you know the answer."

My voice is sharp with dislike. "Assassins. And what about this place?"

His gaze flicks to my chin, but he doesn't try to touch me. "It's called a Realm. It's created by assassin's magic." He points to his ring. "All assassins have rings, but I'm the only one allowed to wear mine in the Realm, which is lucky. Otherwise your fight might have gone differently."

I retort, "I don't think so."

He ignores my arrogant response. Okay, it was a bit brash, but I'd rather believe that I could beat them than not.

He continues, "All Realms are invisible to the outside world. The Horde's Realm occupies the same space as the Texas Capitol. You can only enter it with permission, which I gave you when I brought you with me."

He gestures to the room around us. "This building is called a Cathedral. It's the Master Assassin's home."

He pauses. "It's ... *my* home."

I continue to press the ice against my jaw, exhaling my frustration about what happened. "Cain ... you should have told me that you're the Master. When those assholes tried to push Parker around, I could have protected her with words, not fists."

He is quiet. "You showed me that you're willing to put your life on the line for Parker. I should have known you would, after what you did for Briar this morning. You protected Parker and you saved Briar's life. I owe you for that. I have a lot of secrets, but I should have trusted you."

My anger deflates. Since he's being honest with me, I decide to push it one step further. "What did Lutz Logan mean when he said it could have been you?"

Cain folds his arms across his chest, but the way his expression saddens tells me it's a protective gesture, not an angry one. "When Briar broke our Code, one of us was required to carry out her assassination. It would have fallen to me if Lutz hadn't stepped up."

I'm starting to think the code he follows is completely screwed up.

I sigh. "Why did you bring us here, Cain? What reason could you possibly have to expose Parker to all of this?"

His arms unfold. "I had no choice. The Cathedral is the safest place in the Realm, protected by magic that will incinerate anyone who tries to enter without permission. That's why I had to leave you outside so I could lower the protective spells. It's also why I had to bring you here. Grace ... you need to know..."

His voice fades. My ears buzz. I miss what he says as darkness bleeds into my vision and ringing fills my ears. I've ignored it for too long in my quest for answers and now it overtakes me with vengeance.

I grip the baton harder, but it doesn't work. Despite everything, I don't want to be vulnerable in front of Cain. Stupid pride won't let me ask for help. My stupid heart is worried he'll see me as a burden. I'm nobody's burden.

His voice becomes far away. "Grace?"

My grip on the baton fails. As soon as it slips out of my hands, the burn in my shoulders flares like someone has lit me on fire. I gasp in a breath, stumble, reach out in the air, and swivel left, dropping the ice pack as I go.

Bedroom. Bed.

My hand shoots up—*stop*—as Cain tries to follow me.

His forehead crinkles with alarm, but I won't let him come after me.

I manage, "No. Leave me be."

I reach the door, catch the handle, push it closed, take another step, and hit the floor.

So much for making it to the bed. But as my head touches the carpet, the darkness doesn't overtake me after all.

For the first time, I want it. I need it, because the searing pain in my back is killing me. I try to breathe, gulp air, afraid I'm going to stop breathing. I've experienced a lot of pain, but this is bad. Like being set on fire bad.

It rips through me, shattering my sense of self, trying to pull me apart from the inside. I curl up, unable to stop the tears streaming down my cheeks or the sobs I try to stifle with my hand. A force builds along my spine, pushing from within like something trying to get out and it ... *burns.*

Oh, please, it has to stop.

The door bursts open. "Grace!"

Cain storms into the room, wraps his arms around me, and picks me up.

The moment he touches me, the agony stops.

I gasp a pain-free breath, my eyes shooting wide at how suddenly it disappeared. I hiccup, gulp, and try to see his face.

He is intent on carrying me to the bed, shifting his balance to place me on it, but I cling to him like a cat about to be dropped into water.

The pain stopped when he picked me up. I don't

know why, but I can't let it come back. I don't think I'll survive it.

I'm ready to wrap my legs around him if I have to. "Don't let me go!"

He pauses. "Grace?"

"I can't explain, but please … don't stop touching me."

He lowers me onto the bed but I refuse to release him, curling my fists into his shirt and forcing him to come with me. He ends up lying half beside me and half under me, my chest pressed to his and my right arm pinned beneath his broad torso. It will go numb in this position, but it's a consequence I'm willing to take.

As he brushes the hair out of my eyes, his ring glows. It leaves a soothing trail across my cheek, and I suddenly wonder…

It's the ring. It has to be. The assassin's magic made the pain stop.

His voice is a low rumble, compelling me to answer him. "Grace, please tell me what's going on."

Truth is hard, but somehow I manage to speak it. "This happens after a fight. I pass out. But only if I fight with a weapon. It doesn't matter what the weapon is. Gun, knife … baton." I try to smile, but fail. "When I hold a weapon in my hand, I get calm. Nobody can beat me. But afterward, I pay the price."

He asks, "Is that what happened this morning? You fought Lutz and then you collapsed."

"It used to take much longer to hit me. But now it's minutes after the fight stops."

"What about on the floor just now? What was that?"

I say, "I've never felt that before. That pain ... in my shoulders ... it was intense."

He twists, lifting me a little. "May I take a look?"

I hesitate. "Okay, but don't—"

"I won't stop touching you."

He places a hand on my waist, lifting himself so I can extricate my arm from under him and rise to a kneeling position beside him. Then he sits up, positioning both hands at my waist, skimming my body as I turn around on the bed so my back is to him. I lift my shirt up over my head and scrunch it in my lap. Little shivers make my toes curl as his fingertips travel gently up to my shoulder blades.

I hold my breath. "What do you see?"

He pauses. Then he says, "Your skin is…"

"What, Cain? Please, I'm a little scared right now, and believe me when I say it takes a lot to scare me."

He is deadly serious as he says, "I know, Grace. You are fierce and protective. I don't mean to keep you in suspense. I'm finding the words. Your skin is a different color here." He presses each of his palms flat against my shoulder blades.

I suppress the rising panic, focusing on his touch instead. "What color?"

"Copper."

I nearly jolt out of his hold. "You mean like … *orange?*"

His tone is soothing. "No, burnished gold. Like a sunset. But only across your shoulders."

"Well, that's…" *Weird and unusual.* "It must be bruising."

Except that Brenna only hit me on one side. I promptly ignore that thought.

He responds with, "Hmm."

His fingertips travel outward across my shoulders. He pauses at my left shoulder and murmurs, "This wound was meant for Parker, wasn't it?"

It's the place Brenna hit me with the baton.

Cain shifts closer, his knees moving to either side of my hips as he presses a light kiss against the wound.

He says, "Thank you."

Any reply I might have made evaporates. His lips are soft and the unexpected contact kicks my heart rate up a thousand percent. Despite what must be a growing bruise, the sensation running through that part of my body is anything but pain. I can't find my voice as his other hand trails down my spine.

I close my eyes, allowing myself to soak up his touch. Being touched like this … like every part of my back is worth exploring … isn't something I've experience before. Sex with Jeremy was very much a basic in and out kind of process, leaving me wanting something I couldn't reach. I convinced myself I was okay with it, that being with someone took time, that I would figure out how my body works. Eventually. Maybe.

But between fighting me this morning—if I can even call it fighting—and tending to my wounds, Cain has already touched me more thoroughly than Jeremy ever did.

It scares me.

I've made myself vulnerable to him in more ways than I ever intended. He controls the roof over my head and my safety. I can't let him get close to my heart too.

I whisper, "I think it's safe for you to let me go now."

He makes another one of those non-committal "hmm" noises.

Then he asks, "What if I would like to *not* let you go?"

His touch is light, gentle. I close my eyes, soaking up the sensations as his hands brush slowly back and forth along my spine, up across my shoulders, and down my arms.

I spin so fast that he blinks.

Then he smiles. I'm still firmly ensconced between his knees. His hands lifted away from me as soon as I moved, allowing me to turn, but now they slide safely back around my waist. A very uncompromising place to hold me.

He says, "I need to keep touching you, Grace ... because I have to take care of those stitches. I also want to put some ice on your shoulder right away."

He arches an eyebrow at me, challenging me to read anything else into his intentions.

I narrow my eyes at him, but it's not because of the way he touched me. My chin has stopped bleeding; my stitches can wait, because I missed his explanation before about why we're here. "Why did you bring us here, Cain? Really?"

His smile fades. "The phone call I got in the car. It was Briar."

"Briar! Is she okay?"

"Yes, she's safe, but she wanted to warn me. Lady Tirelli's people are mobilizing. Word is out that Archer Ryan—*you*—have resurfaced. Lady Tirelli can't afford to let you challenge her. On top of that, Lutz is hot on your trail. Simply being in my territory is not enough to protect you anymore. This is your only safe place."

I contemplate him. There's more. Something he's not telling me. "But...?"

He fixates on the floor for a moment. Then he shakes himself. "There is no 'but.' Please stay with me until we know what we're dealing with."

I won't give up my freedom or my control, but his concern is valid. The minute I outed myself in Boston, I put myself in danger. I bite my lip, answering him carefully: "Given that every assassin in this place wants to kill me, I'm not sure this really is the safest place."

His response is emphatic. "Even if they wanted to hurt you, they can't. The Assassin's Code dictates when we can and can't kill. To break the code means death. Besides, I've added extra protective spells around my quarters."

The corner of his mouth lifts. His gaze drops to my lips. "And … I told them you're my woman. They don't expect you to leave my bedroom."

My lips part, a retort the only response I can make: "I will stay with you, but I won't hide."

He leans over and drops a kiss on my bare shoulder. "I don't expect you to."

Before I can process his touch, he slips off the bed and prowls into the kitchen, returning with a medical-grade ice pack—a gel one that won't melt—cloth bandages, and a medical kit. I'm relieved that the pain in my back hasn't returned. I'm in the process of pulling my shirt back on, but he halts me.

"You need this directly against your skin. Here. Lie down on your right side for me."

I eye him but do as he asks. He quickly sets about positioning the pack against my left shoulder, carefully bandaging it in place so it defies gravity. The cool sensation is welcome against my skin.

Cain kneels beside the bed and checks over my face. "I was worried the stitches had pulled out, but they're intact."

He opens the medical kit and sets to work cleaning the wound. My eyes close as he concentrates. The touch of his other hand is light against my cheek and neck. Every now and then he brushes my hair back, his fingertips stroking through the strands around my face and neck, lulling me to sleep. I forget that I'm only wearing a black t-shirt bra. I'm surprised to realize that I don't feel embarrassed or exposed.

Eventually, he says quietly. "All done. You've had a long day. You should get some rest."

He pulls up a blanket. It settles over me like a cloud. *Oh boy, these are definitely expensive blankets.* Nothing like the scratchy old one I had.

I can barely keep my eyes open. It's unusual for me to relax so completely, which makes me suspect Cain had something to do with it. I didn't notice his assassin's ring glow like it did when he subdued Parker, but I ask, "Did you do that thing to me? What you did to help Parker sleep?"

I catch the smile in his voice when he says, "No. Whatever you feel right now, it's all you."

I rouse myself enough to ask, "Will Parker be okay?"

"She'll be fine while I'm gone."

My eyes flash open. "Where are you going?"

He pauses in the process of standing up. "I have to deal with the assassins. I won't be long."

I settle back onto the pillow. I've been alone for years. It doesn't bother me if he takes off. But I have to admit ... I won't be sorry when he comes back.

CHAPTER EIGHT

A confusing amount of light glows behind my eyelids when I wake, together with an equally confusing warm body next to mine. I usually wake up with freezing toes, but the soles of my feet are happily pressed against a warm pair of calves. Deciding not to make any sudden moves, I crack open my eyelids the tiniest bit to see what I'm contending with.

No help at all. I'm facing away from him.

My eyes are gritty and dry. I don't normally sleep wearing my contact lenses. No matter what happens, I can't show Cain my eyes. I can't show anyone.

Refusing to rub my eyes, I roll over very slowly, trying not to shake the bed.

Cain's deep breathing remains unbroken. His dark eyelashes rest against his cheeks and his lips are relaxed. One arm rests outside the blanket, the sleeve of his white t-shirt pulling across his large bicep. He isn't lying as close to me as I thought. In fact, I was the one who extended my feet toward him.

Poor, cold feet. Not their fault.

His rumbly voice startles me. "I put Parker in the spare bed. I tried the couch, but I couldn't get to sleep."

His eyes remain closed. His breathing remains even. He's so still that I start to believe I imagined him speaking.

"Cain?"

His green eyes slowly open. "I'll get out if you want."

I swallow the lump in my throat. "It's your bed. I should sleep on the couch tonight."

He relaxes. "Hmm. Nope."

As if my response gave him permission, he reaches over and scoops me toward him, tucking me into his side so that I'm facing him. "If someone barges in, they'll think it's strange if you're on the couch."

The press of his body is like electricity through me. My breath catches, then speeds up. I hide it by tipping my head back in indignation. "I thought you said nobody could get in here."

Unperturbed by my accusation, he strokes one hand down my back, resting it on my upper thigh, where it warms my body. His other arm tucks under my shoulder and his hand curls up into my hair, cradling the back of my head.

His eyes change color in the morning light, his gaze deepening. His focus shifts to my lips, his own curling up at one corner in a lazy smile. "There goes that excuse, then."

My stomach fills with beating wings. My heart stutters. Being held like this, totally sheltered in his arms, feels both powerfully safe and intensely danger-ous. My back is arched to allow me to meet his eyes, our chests smooshed together, my hips pressed against his. I fight the need to hook my upper leg around his hips and draw him closer—as close as we were yesterday when we did that dance I'd prefer to call "fighting."

He takes a deep breath but doesn't make another move. He closes his eyes again, seeming content to stay just as he is. I'm not sure what to do with this. His nearness sends all sorts of messages into parts of my body that should not be awake right now. Parts of my body I can't listen to or I'll make my situation way more complicated than it needs to be.

His chest expands as he takes a deep breath, his eyes still closed. "What do you like to eat for breakfast?"

Talking is good. Talking is safe. "Toast."

His lips part in a chuckle that rumbles around in his chest. "Just toast?"

I swallow. "It's cheap."

"Grace ... not what do you eat for breakfast. What would you *like* to eat for breakfast? If you could have anything?"

I allow myself to smile, not believing for a minute that he'll take me seriously. "A blueberry muffin and a mocha latte."

"Consider it done."

Before I can draw breath, he gathers me up against him, rolls onto his back so I'm lying on top of him, pulls my legs around his hips, and lifts off the bed while I cling to him in a position that I never imagined being in fully clothed.

I fight every impulse to arch into him, to drop my weight back onto the bed and take him with me. I focus intently on the shadow across his jaw to stifle my instincts as he walks to the bathroom, supporting me in that position.

He says, "Let's check your wound."

All business, he props me on the bathroom counter, running his palm across my cheek to tilt my face so he can examine my chin. His fingertips brush my earlobe and ... I'm done hiding the effect he has on me.

I sigh at the sensation, allowing my eyes to close, refusing to fight how it makes me feel—alive and calm at the same time.

He murmurs, "It looks much better than I thought

it would. Sarah came by last night and took a quick look while you were sleeping. She'll check you over again today to make sure."

As the breath draws in and out of my lungs and his hand remains where it is, there is a moment of stillness.

Then...

"Grace." His thumb brushes across my cheek for a moment, his palm sliding out from beside my ear, allowing his fingertips to reach my lips. He traces the outline of my bottom lip in a tingling movement.

He asks, "How are you so perfect?"

My eyes flash open. "Are you mocking me?"

He is focused, serious, his own lips slightly parted, a gentle frown resting on his forehead. "Never."

His expression loses nothing of its intensity as he says, "Sarah will take Parker to the apartment and stay with her there. I'm sorry you need to remain here, but ... I want you to come out into the Realm with me. I'll show you everything, tell you everything about this place. And if you want..." He smiles suddenly. "I'll show you how I beat you yesterday."

There's a challenge in his gaze that I can't ignore— it's an expression he wears often when he looks at me, as if he's daring me...

Actually, I'm not sure what he's daring me to do, but I'm determined to figure it out.

I tip my chin, inadvertently turning my cheek into

his palm. If there's anything perfect in my life, it's the way his thumb rests against the corner of my lips, sending tingles to my toes.

I manage to say, "You didn't beat me. I let you win."

He says, "We'll see." In the next breath he continues: "You'll find clean clothes on the counter. I guessed your size. Your bag is there, too. Take as long as you want. Breakfast will be waiting when you get out."

He's gone within moments, closing the door behind him.

I rush to strip off my shirt, trying to see my shoulder blades and the strange golden color he described yesterday, but everything looks normal. It must have been early bruising.

Then I pounce on my shoulder bag, digging out the little box containing my spare contact lenses, along with the special solution to clean them.

Leaning over the basin, I slide out my current lenses, blinking my eyes with relief. *Thank goodness.* I can leave them out while I shower.

I freeze when I glance in the mirror. I don't recognize myself.

The color of my eyes changes my face.

I look ... different.

Not normal.

Dad's voice thunders in my memory. I rub my neck, remembering his meaty fist like a vise around my throat when I forgot to put in my contact lenses one morning. But at least it wasn't a cigarette butt on my arm. He shoved me against the wall, cracking my head against it, shouting, *Stupid girl! Put your fucking contacts in. Show anyone your eyes and I'll fucking kill you.*

He's no longer here to kill me, but I learned my lesson: distinguishing marks are memorable.

Memorable is dangerous.

Violet eyes are … unforgettable.

CHAPTER NINE

I wash off the memories, emerging from the shower feeling in control again. The clothes Cain gave me fit surprisingly well—fitted jeans with lots of stretch for movement, brand new underwear, and a navy-blue shirt that's equally soft. I'm not sure whether I should feel uncomfortable about the fact that the bra is exactly the right size, but I'm pretty sure the tag on my bra was visible yesterday after I took my shirt off.

My sense of peace disappears the minute I enter the lounge room, where the air is tense. I find Parker looking less than happy, a deep frown on her face, her arms folded over her chest. She's dressed but her hair is mussed up. She perches on the edge of the couch as if she would rather be standing. Or possibly shouting.

Cain sits opposite, leaning forward, elbows on his knees, hands clasped. He *looks* relaxed, but the tension around his mouth and eyes tell a different story.

I'm pretty sure they had a whole conversation while I was in the shower that must have involved the truths that Cain has been concealing from Parker ever since he met her.

Parker holds out her hand for me as soon as she sees me, drawing me onto the couch to sit beside her. Her fingertips close tightly around mine, unexpectedly protective. "So Grace is stuck here, surrounded by a bunch of vicious assassins—for whom you're apparently the big boss—and I'm supposed to be okay with abandoning her."

"It's the best option."

"For whom? You didn't see what they tried to do to her yesterday. I did!"

"That won't happen again."

Parker shakes her head at him vehemently. Her hand tightens around mine. "Grace is the only reason I'm in one piece today. She can't stay here with these people. And neither should you, Cain."

Cain contemplates the carpet, his lips pressed together. He finally raises his eyes to hers. "This is where I belong. These are my people."

Her face falls. The way she blinks rapidly, biting her lip, tells me how upset she is. Close to tears. "I don't buy that for a second. I know you, Cain. This is not you."

Cain is still calm. Never angry. "You don't know me as well as you think you do, Parker."

She sucks in a sharp breath. "And you don't know Grace. Not at all. But you've dragged her here, the same as me, because neither of us has anywhere else to go. Now you get to decide what happens to us." She swallows, tears dripping down her cheeks. "That's not fair."

He nods. "It's not."

"And you're right. You kill people. I don't know you at all."

I stare at Parker's hand on mine. She wouldn't be so protective if she knew who I was and what I've done.

I whisper, "I have, too."

The first sign of alarm flashes across Cain's face. "Grace, no. You don't have to…"

I turn to Parker, meeting her shocked eyes. "I deserve what I get. This place is filled with killers and now it has an extra one."

She stutters, "I … no … you protected me…"

"Because you deserve better. Please don't be angry at Cain on my behalf. I've never known a different life. But you … you have the sweetest soul I have ever met. You deserve amazing things."

Despite what I said, she hasn't let go of my hand. She asks, "That guy yesterday?"

"An assassin," I say. "He's coming after me. If he finds me, I'm dead. Apparently he can't set foot inside this place, so this is where I have to remain."

She finally pulls her hand away from mine.

I let her go, a widening hole in my heart.

She says, "I think I'll wait in my room until Sarah gets here."

Cain stands up when she leaves, but he doesn't try to stop her.

He clears his throat in the silence that surrounds us. "Grace, you should eat."

He gestures to the kitchen table, where a blueberry muffin rests on a plate with a bowl of fruit and a chocolate-sprinkled coffee beside it. Along with toast.

He got me the breakfast of my dreams. And now ... I don't know how I'll eat it. How I'll eat anything. I say, "Thank you" even though it sounds hollow in my ears.

He is subdued as he sits with me, not even a glimmer of a smile. There's a visible weight across his shoulders. "You're welcome."

Halfway through the meal, his assassin's ring gleams. He suddenly pushes back his seat, strides to the door, and opens it to reveal Sarah standing outside.

She raises her eyebrows in a questioning look. "Parker?"

He shakes his head. "It didn't go well."

She doesn't look surprised. "It's impossible for her to feel safe here. I'll check over Grace and then get Parker to the apartment. It will help once she's back in a normal routine with a normal environment." As she makes her way inside, she adds, "The apartment is beautiful, Cain. Thank you."

Cain stays out of the way as Sarah pulls up a chair in front of me. "How are you feeling, Grace?"

"I'm fine. Just feeling…" I glance at Cain. The hole in my heart is a nasty, dark pit. Having Parker around was like having a normal relationship for the very first time. Now it's gone. I swallow the emotions. "I'm fine."

She frowns as she looks over my chin. "Your skin has knitted already. Normally, I would leave the stiches in for a few days, but I should take them out now or you're more likely to scar."

Cain leans forward. "Already?"

I retain a blank expression. "I've always healed fast."

Sarah says, "Okay, well … I've seen stranger things. Let's get the stitches out."

She leads me to Cain's bedroom, giving Cain a small smile before she firmly closes the door.

Then she says, "I'm not sure how far sound travels in this place and Parker doesn't need to hear our conversation."

She opens her bag and pulls out multiple sterilized

packets of implements. "You did well to fend off Brenna yesterday. Cain told me you have skills, but beating her is impressive."

I don't feel even remotely proud right now. "What is Brenna's position here?"

Sarah's lips thin as she sets to work. "She is Cain's second in command."

"Wait ... that means she's in charge?"

"When he's not around. Which has been for months now. The power has gone to her head."

"Please tell me he didn't choose her?"

"I'm afraid he did." Sarah gives me a wry smile. "It's a case of keep your enemies close."

I sigh. "I see."

I lie still while Sarah works over me. She explains, "A new Master is chosen every twenty years. Brenna wanted to be the first female Master, but Cain's final mission blew her out of contention. He completed five kills in one night. It was a record in the assassin's world."

I decide not to mention the fact that I've killed more thugs in a night than that. The night Dad died, to be exact. I shake off the memory, the pain, the battle, my loyalty to him stopping me from running when I should have. After that, I didn't stop running.

As Sarah finishes up, I ask, "There's never been a female Master?"

"Not of a Faction. But there have been several

formidable female assassins in our history. One lived in Boston as a matter of fact. They called her the Glass Fox."

I force myself to remain relaxed. "What happened to her?"

"Nobody knows how she died. But it must have been foul play, because she was a truly powerful assassin. She only relinquished her chance to be Master of the Legion because she became pregnant with a daughter she needed to protect."

I chew my lip. What Sarah said confirms what I haven't wanted to acknowledge: my father was mixed up in the world of assassins, and his fiercest protector, who died hours before him, was the only reason he remained alive. She handed him the keys to the underworld and annihilated his competition.

But why would she ally herself with him? I don't understand what a woman that powerful could gain from helping a man like my father. Sure, he was my Dad, but he was a brute, a thug no better than the ones she killed for him.

I also didn't know she had a daughter. It means that somewhere out there is a woman who lost her mother the same night I lost Dad.

Sarah says, "Technically, Cain isn't Master yet. He's currently the Heir Apparent. Now that he has returned from Boston, he has to stay here permanently. He will be formally recognized in a week. It's going to be hard for him to care for Parker after that."

"I'm glad she has you."

Sarah gives me a genuine smile. "Those two have got their hooks into my heart, that's for sure."

"I assume you're an assassin, too?"

Her smile grows. "Of course. But these days I save lives, not take them. I've been the head physician at the Horde for many years, but I'll pass my title on in a week. It's my job to look after Parker now."

Sarah pats my shoulder before she rises, opens the door, and heads back to the kitchen. I stay where I am, swinging my legs over the edge of the bed. I want to say goodbye to Parker, but it's better if I stay out of the way.

I perch on the side of the bed, waiting long moments until I hear the door open and close again. I exhale, trying to focus on what's ahead of me now. Staying here. Living in this place. Until it's safe for me to leave.

Cain appears in the doorway. "You didn't have to tell Parker the truth."

"Yes, I did. I can't lie to her. Just like I can't lie to you."

He doesn't ask me why. There are a lot of things he doesn't ask me.

I continue, "There's an immediate threat to my life,

which means I need to stay in this place. But I won't stay here forever, Cain. I can't."

For once he doesn't give me his usual "hmm."

"I know. It's just for now." He is quiet. Then he exhales. "I need to get changed. Then I'd like to show you the Realm."

CHAPTER TEN

*C*ain reappears dressed in his own version of khaki uniform: cargo pants and a t-shirt that stretches across his muscled chest and biceps. Four daggers disappear into various pockets around his person, each one etched with a symbol that looks like two C's back to back. I guess, like Slade, Cain gets his own daggers. The one I took from Lutz Logan is hidden in the bottom of my bag, and I intend to leave it there until I figure out a way to get rid of it.

We head outside the cathedral and Cain shows me the Realm's layout and the quarters where the other assassins live. He explains that only a small portion of the Horde's assassins live here—mostly only the trainees and teachers. And him. He tells me that after he is officially the Master, he can come and go, but the Realm becomes his home. He also explains that the former Master already lives outside of the Realm to allow Cain to establish control. The way he describes the previous Master tells me that Cain respects him.

He says, "I chose this life before I knew about Parker. Even if I could go back in time..." He shakes his head. "I can't deny who I am."

He takes me around the combat rooms, each purposed for different training. I let out a wry laugh at the elongated room for indoor archery.

"I tried archery once, but it didn't go so well. You'd think I'd be good at it, wouldn't you?"

He gives me a sharp look. "You aren't your name, Archer."

It's the first time he's called me that since we arrived. The way he says it ... it doesn't sound so bad.

After that, I follow Cain to the sparring, room where the trainees—the "Novices"—grapple with each other as they learn everything from wrestling to kickboxing.

Cain says, "The Horde's intake is later than the other Factions, so these Novices still have two months left in their training."

I recognize the group from yesterday—except for one woman. She is much smaller than the others, thin with lank hair and dark circles under her eyes. The trainee she wrestles is twice her size and has no problem annihilating the hell out of her.

As soon as they see Cain, the trainees stop what

they're doing and stand to attention, arms spread out at their sides, fingers splayed.

"Master," they chime together.

He waves them back to what they were doing.

I murmur to Cain, "Why do they greet you like that?"

"To show they don't carry weapons against me. Each Faction has different traditions. The Legion bows to their Master but they never take their eyes off each other."

I was expecting a frosty reception from the trainees, a repeat of the aggression they showed me yesterday, but their faces are drawn, their shoulders down.

I say, "They look tired."

"I sent them to volunteer in a soup kitchen to serve those in need. They've been awake since four o'clock this morning. They will serve again tomorrow. One way or another, I will teach them compassion."

My eyebrows rise. "Assassins who value compassion?"

"You probably think of us as cold-blooded killers for hire, but we never act unless the justice system has failed. Even then, every assassination must be sanctioned by the Guardian. She is our gatekeeper. She never sanctions a mission unless it's justified. Our clients are heartbroken people who have nowhere else to turn. But ... I won't deny that this place attracts those whose blood runs cold. Otherwise, we couldn't do what we do."

I soften my voice. "What about you, Cain?"

His gaze becomes distant. "There's darkness in me, Grace. Make no mistake. That's all you need to know."

When he doesn't elaborate, I have to accept that it's the only answer he is willing to give me.

I point to the small woman who wasn't with the group yesterday. When her sparring partner flips her onto her back, she winces, rolls over, and gets up again, facing off with him, her expression resigned.

I ask, "Who is that?"

Cain takes a moment to consider her, a frown growing on his forehead. "That's Juliet. She excels at poisons. Otherwise she would have been sent home a long time ago."

Cold anger floods me. "Just because a woman is little doesn't mean it's okay to push her around. Her inability to defend herself is a failing on the part of her teacher, not her."

"I agree with you, Grace. But this life isn't suited to everyone..."

I choose to hear the first thing he said and not the second. If I were to look deeper into my motivations, I'd have to recognize that I'm still stinging about what happened with Parker, but right now I'm throwing caution to the wind. "Since you agree with me, I'm going to do something about it."

Without waiting for his okay, I stride onto the floor, headed for the girl.

The trainees around me immediately scramble out of the way, jumping to their feet and standing to attention as fast as they can.

They shout, "Mistress on the floor!"

Mistress, huh?

I head straight to the big guy. He was the one who asked Brenna if she needed help yesterday. He was also the one who kneed me in the back. He might have spent his morning helping others, but arrogance burns behind his insolent expression as he eyes my approach.

I stop and level my gaze with him. He is tall, but not as much as Cain, which means that I'm at eye-height with him.

I ask, "How's your leg, Novice?"

I had swept his standing leg out from under him. I'm sure he has a nasty bruise on his calf today.

His jaw clenches. "Fine, Mistress."

"Then get out of my way." I glare at him a moment longer: *You are not worth my time.*

He steps aside to reveal Juliet struggling to get to her feet. Up close I can see that she's bruised everywhere—her arms, legs, neck, cheekbone, chin. On top of that, her lip is split, and I can only imagine how her ribs are faring.

I would hold out my hand for her, but any pressure

will hurt her right now. "Come with me please, Juliet. I will train you from now on."

An outraged gasp draws my attention. Brenna pulls herself off the wall. Until now she has stayed in the background, her arms folded tightly across her chest.

She says, "I don't think so."

I stand my ground. "Show me one technique you've taught this woman."

Brenna glances at Juliet. She takes a little too long to reply. I guess she's coming up blank.

"Or have you not bothered because of her physique?" My blood is boiling. "Because small women will never be able to defend themselves against giant brutes, will they?"

She scowls. "You have no right to take over my training room."

I shoot back. "I will not interfere with your teaching since you aren't training this woman at all. In fact, I'm doing you a favor. She is one less body to worry about."

"Fine! Take her away. She's useless anyway."

I spin to Juliet, lowering my voice. "Come with me, please."

Juliet shoots wide eyes between me and Brenna. She doesn't know me, but I hope she heard about what happened yesterday, including the part where I kicked Brenna's butt. She gives me a nod and follows me to the door.

I pause beside Cain, challenging him to stop me.

He wears a faint smile. He looks almost … impressed.

The appreciation in his eyes warms me a little more than I'm used to. I clear my throat, remaining frosty. "If I have to stay, then I need something to do."

His smile grows. "I won't stop you." But it fades when he says to Juliet, "Halt, Novice."

She pulls up sharp and plasters her gaze to the floor.

He places a light finger under her chin so he can examine her face without hurting her. "When did this start?"

Her voice is surprisingly melodious, a sweet wash of sound that makes me look closer. Under the dirt, her hair is light brown with a touch of auburn, and her eyes are a deep blue with silver flecks. She could be gorgeous under all those bruises.

She says, "Right after you left for Boston, Master."

I jump in to the conversation with a growl at Cain. "Just as well. If I thought this was happening under your watch, Cain Carter, I would…"

I want to tell him that he would answer to me, but actually, there's not a lot I could do except glare daggers at him the same way Brenna is glaring at me.

He gives me a broad smile, one that makes my stomach flutter. "You'd what, woman? Make me sleep on the couch?"

I can't stop the heat filling my cheeks. "I need a private training room and as many icepacks as you can give me."

He switches gears surprisingly fast. "Follow me."

I draw level with Juliet as we hurry to keep up with Cain along the footpath.

I say to her, "We need to treat your wounds first, then we can train."

She fires at me, "I don't want your pity."

I appreciate her pride. I respond firmly: "You won't get any. What you will gain from me is instruction. Listen to what I say and you'll put that idiot on his butt in a week's time."

She lets out a short laugh. "That's impossible."

I find myself channeling Cain's favorite response, the one he uses when he wants to disagree with me. "Hmm. No."

Cain takes us to a quiet section of the Realm—a beautiful historical building that was hidden from my view before. "This is the guest house. You can use the training room on the lower level. I'll have ice brought to you."

He swings on his heels and I venture along the corridor until we reach a large room containing mats and dummies. No weapons on the walls, but that's okay for now.

When Cain returns, he is followed by a staff member hauling a trolley with a box of icepacks.

Cain leans against the doorway, arms folded across his broad chest. "All the ice packs I can give you."

"Thank you."

Without fuss, I set about bandaging them to the worst of Juliet's bruises.

When I finish, she asks, quieter now, "If it's not pity, then … why are you doing this?"

I want to tell her the truth: because I can do something about her situation when I can't do anything about my own.

Instead, I say, "Because … I like to piss Brenna off."

She lets out a laugh and then covers it, shooting a wary glance at Cain, who hasn't budged from the doorway.

I sit down opposite her on a mat. I spend the next hour talking to her about how she moves and how she can compensate for her opponent's height and weight. She listens, and when she's ready, I bandage her hands to protect her knuckles and get her to stand up and practice her punches with one of the dummies, correcting her balance as she proceeds.

Cain comes and goes, seeming content to leave us be.

Until I glance up and realize that it must be lunchtime.

Juliet is much more relaxed now. She says, "I have magic and poisons classes in the afternoons. Will I come back here tomorrow morning for combat training?"

"Seven a.m. sharp, please."

"Thank you, Mistress."

She splays her arms before exiting the room.

Cain lumbers over to me. "You're a born teacher."

I shrug. "That sounds like a compliment, Cain."

He continues, "But you're missing an element of combat." He arches an eyebrow in a way I recognize as a challenge. "I said I'd show you how I beat you."

I square my shoulders and take up position in the middle of the floor. It's a sprung floor with multiple padded mats scattered around for safe tumbling. It's nowhere near as harsh an environment as I assumed an assassin's training camp would be. "Go ahead."

He takes up position a careful two paces from me. "You either attack or defend, but you always move with impact. I assume that's the way you were taught. But defeating your opponent isn't only about making an impression, it's also about containment."

I remember the way Cain avoided my strikes and fought back by restraining instead of attacking me. "You ... contained me."

He tips his chin at me. "I did a good job of it, too."

"Hah! Try it again, *Master*."

He blinks at me, clearly thrown.

I take advantage of his distraction to step up and take a swing at him. He sidesteps me but I'm ready for that move, quickly spinning, but this time my hand grazes his torso as I pass by. He catches my hand and spins me back to him, but I glide under his arm, catching and dragging him just slightly toward me. He turns with me, taking a step forward, moving with me.

For the next five minutes, we turn and move in a sort of fight-dance, neither one of us gaining a hold on the other until I decide to let down my defenses, tugging him toward me, chest-to-chest, allowing his arms to fold around me. We slow and stop in that position.

Being contained by Cain is not so bad.

He murmurs, "You adapted."

Feeling pleased with myself, I tip my head, my hair sliding to the side. "Always learn your opponent."

He catches my eye. Then he drops a kiss on the side of my exposed neck. It's the briefest contact. He pulls back, but only a little, his lips close to mine and a hint of dare back in his brilliant eyes.

I find myself wondering ... would it be so terrible if I closed the gap and kissed him?

Yes, it would. Remember where you are and why you're here.

Hating my inner logic, I pull away. I'm not sure if my heart or my body can take more close encounters with Cain Carter.

CHAPTER ELEVEN

*M*y belongings arrive that evening—all two boxes of them. One contains my clothing. The other is filled with books. If I had left Boston by myself, I would have been forced to leave my books behind.

After my shower, I search for the linen cupboard, determined to make up the spare bed to sleep in it. I drag my boxes into the spare room. Then I finish changing the sheets, smoothing out the surface.

"Grace?" Cain's call is short, sharp, an urgent edge to it that I haven't heard before.

I shoot upright, calling back, "I'm in here."

He appears in the doorway, dressed only in boxer shorts, water dripping from his hair and down his bare chest as if he didn't stop to dry himself properly.

I brace, preparing for a disaster or an attack. "What's wrong?"

"It was quiet. You weren't in the living room, so I thought…" He inhales. Stops speaking. Folds his arms across his chest and then unfolds them.

I study him with surprise. "You thought I left without telling you."

"It's possible."

I draw myself upright, wanting to ease his worry but not sure how. "Cain … I can't stay here forever, but I won't ghost on you."

He rolls his shoulders as if he's easing the tension out of them. Then he studies the turned-down bed. "What are you doing?"

"Getting ready to sleep."

"In here?"

I turn away from him to plump the pillow, happy with how the bed turned out. "Uh-huh."

There's a pause behind me. Then … "No."

"Huh?" My question ends up muffled against his chest as he appears beside me and picks me up, easily hoisting me into his arms, hooking my legs around his waist while I'm still holding the pillow. I end up startled, frozen, the pillow wedged against his side, and as close to him as I was this morning.

His arms tighten, his voice gruff in my ears. "You should sleep in my room so that I'm close by if something happens. I don't want to lose anyone else I care about."

It hits me that he's talking about losing Parker. He hasn't spoken about her all day. My hurt at losing her friendship is nothing compared to his. He has so much more to lose if she doesn't forgive him for who he is.

It's difficult for me to pull back to see his face without making it seem like I'm trying to get free when really ... I'm more comfortable like this than I ever expected to be.

I rest my head against his shoulder, dropping the pillow so I can wrap my arms around him. His big chest rises and falls as he inhales and exhales as if he's measuring his breathing.

I say, "I promise I'm not going anywhere without telling you. Parker was upset, but you're her brother and she loves you more than anything. She won't be angry forever."

He presses his cheek to mine, a rough whisper. "I hope so."

Despite scooping me up, he hasn't moved. He has never dragged me anywhere without my permission and his stillness tells me he won't force me to sleep anywhere I don't want to.

I swallow my emotions, speaking softly against his neck. "I don't mind sleeping in your bed if that's where you need me to be. You make my feet warm."

Without another word, he turns and carries me to

his bed. When he places me down on it, I climb under the blankets without reservation. I wait for him to get in before I scoot over to his side and find his shoulder, the perfect place to rest my head. And his arms, the perfect cocoon around me.

I close my eyes and fall asleep.

For the next four days, I settle into a cautious routine. Juliet is a quick learner and soaks up my instructions. She has skills—she just didn't know how to use them. Within days she's light years ahead of where she was. I spend the afternoons in the archery range, determined to conquer the bow and arrow. Each time, I eventually give up in disgust at my own inability to reliably shoot an arrow and head to the gun range instead, riddling my targets with bullets.

On the fifth morning, two days before Cain's ceremony, I wake to find that he has let me sleep in. What's more, he's not in the bed.

Ouch, my feet are cold.

I pull on socks and emerge into the kitchen to find Sarah at the table with Cain, speaking softly. I'm still in my pajamas, but Cain has seen me like this plenty of times. I ignore Sarah's raised eyebrows. Cain's worried expression tells me there are bigger problems at play than her curiosity about our sleeping arrangements.

"What's going on?" I ask.

He growls, "Lutz Logan."

Sarah leans forward a little, curiosity lighting her eyes. "Cain doesn't want to tell me who you are, Grace. Or what you've done. But Lutz Logan is here for a reason and I need to know why."

I frown at Cain. "I thought he couldn't enter your territory."

"If Slade comes here without permission, I'm entitled to kill him. But Lutz ... well, he can come and go as long as he doesn't get caught."

I spin to Sarah. "Then catch him."

She sighs. "I would if I could, but his reputation is earned. He trained with Slade and that makes him ... unbeatable. I don't dare take him on."

My blood suddenly runs cold. "Has he threatened Parker?"

"No." Sarah is quick to answer, her hand flying upward in a calming gesture. "He hasn't come near her. But he knows where we live. Which makes what I came here to ask much riskier."

"What is it?"

She says, "Parker wants to see you."

I glance at Cain. "Just me? What about Cain?"

Sarah bites her lip. "Sorry. Only you."

Whatever Cain feels about it, he's hiding it well. He is a blank slate right now. I feel guilty about accepting, but it's an olive branch that I can't pass up. "Then I'm going."

Now Cain reacts: "Are you sure that's wise? I brought you here for a reason. It's dangerous out there."

I level my gaze with his. "I beat Lutz before. I'll beat him again. You know I'll keep Parker safe."

Sarah's eyes are wide. "You beat Lutz? When?"

Oops. I wish I could take back my declaration, but it's out there now.

Cain is tight-lipped. He folds his arms across his chest.

I press my own lips together, my jaw clenching. *Stupid mouth.*

Sarah stares at Cain. Then at me. "Other than Hunter Cassidy and Slade Baines, nobody beats Lutz. Unless you're talking about … Archer Ryan…"

She stands up so fast that her chair topples over. "Oh, damn … you're a woman."

I give her a humorless smile and a wave. "Hi."

She presses her palm to her forehead, struggling to focus on me. "Well, this certainly explains why you're here but … Archer Ryan is a killer of … so many … and *damn* Brenna is lucky to be alive."

It's almost comical to see an assassin pale at the idea of how many people I've killed.

"In other words, Grace is pretty damn unbeatable herself." Cain's frown clears as he turns his attention to me. "If you want to go, then you should. The Code makes collateral damage unacceptable, so Lutz won't risk hurting Parker. It's the safest way for you to get out of here for a while."

I say, "I'll get dressed. Oh … but Juliet is expecting me."

Cain stands. "I'll train her this morning. She can put her new skills to the test on someone twice her size."

I glare at him. "Don't intimidate her. Her confidence is still growing. I don't want a setback."

"I don't want her to fail, Grace. As I said, she excels at poisons and her physique makes her the perfect assassin. Some of the most impressive assassinations are the ones nobody knew were kills."

"Okay. I'm trusting you, Cain Carter." But I pause in the doorway, frowning. "Who is Hunter Cassidy?"

Sarah has recovered enough to sit down. "The daughter of the Glass Fox. The one I was telling you about." She pales again. "Oh. But the Glass Fox was the one who protected your father…"

My hand clenches around the doorframe. "Hunter beat Lutz?"

Sarah says, "She's one of the few assassins he doesn't mess with."

Cain leans back in his chair with a dry laugh. "Nobody messes with Hunter."

I allow myself to smile. "Then I like her already."

Parker gives nothing away when she meets me at the door to Cain's apartment. She is dressed casually in jeans and a black sweater that draws out the dark highlights in her hair, but she's also wearing heels and makeup, making me underdressed. Since I got my own clothing back, I've shunned the clothes Cain provided. My clothing leans toward functional instead of pretty. Take my boots, for example, the heels of which can break ribs even though the leather is scuffed beyond belief.

Parker's green eyes remain level with mine. "Apparently you need a dress for the ceremony this Saturday. I'm taking you shopping."

I am completely prepared to let her call the shots today. Whatever she is—or isn't—willing to do or talk about is fine with me. If we keep our conversations to fashion, then … well, actually I probably won't have much to say since dresses are foreign to me.

When she closes the door behind her, I ask, "Sarah isn't coming with us?"

"I asked her not to. It's just you and me."

We travel silently in the car. Every now and then, Spencer glances back at us. I guess the silence is getting to him, too. We travel along the Colorado River and into downtown Austin, stopping in the 2nd Street District. I trail Parker along the sidewalk, hesitating outside the door of a boutique fashion store that Parker confidently leads me to.

I pretend to study the window display as I use the reflection to assess the two guys across the street who have been following us for the last two minutes. I don't recognize them as Horde assassins, although I haven't met all of them so I can't say for sure. Cain could be overprotective. Or they could be Legion. Or they could be Lady Tirelli's people. I won't know for sure until they make a move.

For now, they seem content to watch us.

Inside, the shop contains a glittering array of evening dresses. I can't see price tags, but it doesn't take a genius to know that nothing will cost less than a thousand dollars.

I say, "Parker … I'm happy to try things on, but I can't afford any of this."

She waves a credit card at me. "Cain can."

I frown. "Revenge spending?"

She lowers her eyes. "Actually, no. I have his permission. He wants you to choose something yourself. Or so Sarah told me."

Parker quickly picks out three dresses and propels me toward the dressing room. "Try these on for starters. I'll find more."

The dressing rooms are enormous—large enough to accommodate two women side-by-side in puffy dresses. It's early enough that I'm the only one here. I smooth down the sides of the dress I try on first, jumping when Parker slips a pair of heels under the door and flips a push-up bra over the top. Despite wearing heels, she walks as quietly as her brother.

She calls through the door, "Try these on and come out when you find a dress you like. I'm coming back with more."

I slip on the push-up bra, pull on the heels, and slide on the next dress. It's baby blue with spaghetti straps and an embroidered corset, the fitted skirt overlaid with sheer panels that float down to my toes.

I almost look ... like a woman.

The price tag makes my stomach sink. I could buy a lot of food for that amount.

I reach back to pull the zipper when the corner of the dressing room shifts at the edge of my vision.

I freeze, the back of my neck prickling.

The air shifts again.

Damn. I'm in trouble.

A dangerous voice at my shoulder whispers, "You should stay dressed, sweetheart."

CHAPTER TWELVE

*L*utz Logan materializes right behind me, a menacing form blocking the exit.

I grab the hand he lowers toward my shoulder, twisting and pushing. He drops, following the curve of my push so that I don't break his wrist. He lands on one knee, but his other hand snakes out, catches me behind my own knee, and pulls. At the same time, he maintains hold of my other hand.

I have nowhere to go but down, straddling his bended knee. Right where he wants me. Two big arms whip around me, crushing me close, pinning both of my arms at my sides. Within seconds, he has restrained me and ... damn ... he's strong.

But I still have a trick or two up my sleeve.

I stop struggling and scowl at him. All I need is for him to relax just the smallest amount...

I say, "Since you don't have wings, I assume you were in here the whole time."

His amber eyes crinkle at the corners. His arms shift, but not as much as I want.

He says, "I promise I closed my eyes when you got undressed."

I hiss, "Sure, you did."

He looks genuinely affronted, jerking back from me a little, his arms flexing. It's the only opening I'm going to get. I whip my right leg up and around his hip and drop my weight to the right, forcing him off balance. At the same time, I raise my left knee, using it to leverage him away from me with a shove. I tap his face with my foot on the way, connecting with his mouth. It's not a hard hit, but it has impact.

He bounces to his feet and so do I, but this time we back up against opposite sides of the confined space, facing each other. I'm satisfied to see that his lip is split, but I am unscathed.

Thankfully, so is the dress. An expensive rip is the last thing I need.

His amber eyes follow every movement I make, from the smallest twitch of my fingers to the turn of my head as I consider the door and how fast I might be able to get through it.

He says, "Nice to meet you, Archer Ryan."

It's not nice to meet him. I glare back at him. "What gave it away?"

"Your eyes."

I swallow a laugh. *He has no freaking idea.*

He continues, "And the way Cain whisked you away from Boston. You were a perfect stranger to him but he protected you that day—the same day Archer Ryan rescued Briar. I didn't think any woman could tear Cain away from Hunter. Especially right now when she needs him most."

There's an element of accusation in his tone, as if he disagrees with Cain's choice.

All I hear is "any woman" and "Hunter." Lutz makes it sound as if Cain is bound to Hunter. My voice sharpens. "Hunter Cassidy?"

Lutz's eyes narrow. He considers me for a moment, his expression shifting from angry to curious. And finally his forehead creases with concern. His gaze rakes across my features as if he sees things he doesn't like.

His next question is a goading challenge, laden with implication. "You didn't know about Cain and Hunter?"

I try to keep my expression blank, but my jaw clenches. Cain didn't act as if he and Hunter are together, but if that's the case, then our sleeping arrangements are well and truly inappropriate.

I snap, "Who Cain loves is none of my business."

A deep light of concern floods Lutz's eyes. He loses his offensive stance and drops his weight against the wall, staring at me. *"Damn.* This is way more complicated than I thought it was."

I frown at him, not following his sudden change of gears. "What is?"

He curses again. "You and Cain. I thought he was protecting you because you saved Briar. But if he's protecting you because he loves you … this is not going to end well."

I continue to glare at Lutz. "Cain doesn't love me."

He arches an eyebrow at me. "Keep telling yourself that, sweetheart. But the more important question is: do you love him? Because if you do, you'll come back to Boston with me."

"Why would I do that?"

"Because if you don't, the Code gives Slade the right to kill Cain."

"What?" A shiver runs down my spine. My hands and feet are suddenly numb, my entire body heavy. I lean against the wall for support.

Lutz says, "Nobody wants that to happen. Only you can prevent it."

My blood runs cold. Cain is strong, the most impressive fighter I've ever seen, but he's not invincible. Everything I've heard about Slade tells me that a fight between him and Cain would be … devastating, vicious. Deadly.

Lutz holds out his hand to me. It's like the angel of death asking me to go with him.

I snap upright. I have no reason to believe anything he says. "You're lying."

In response, he growls, "If you don't believe me, then consider this: Lady Tirelli's people are already here. I took care of the two guys tailing you outside the shop. I know you saw them. You were lucky they didn't attack Parker. They don't care who they kill. People will die if you don't come with me. Including Cain."

When I hesitate, he runs his hand through his hair, frustration bleeding into his expression. "Look ... I'm not here to kill you. I'm here to take you back. What happens after that is not in my control."

Whether or not I believe Lutz's story about Slade and Cain, he's right about Parker. I can't let her get hurt. Or Cain for that matter. I know firsthand how brutal the Tirelli Family is, and I've seen what a single bullet can do. Dad was killed by a bullet I didn't see coming.

A bullet I couldn't stop.

Parker ... Cain ... they could be killed, too.

I press my hand against my chest. They are the first people who have ever truly cared about me, took me in without demanding something in return. For a few days, I've had security and happiness.

Now I have to let it go.

But, dammit, I'm going to do it on my own terms.

I snarl, letting my anger out. "I'm dead if I go with

you. I was dead the moment I threw that coffee at you."

He breathes out a slow exhale. "I'm sorry, Archer."

He actually sounds like he means it.

He closes the distance one step at a time, testing me, his amber eyes assessing every twitch I make. He lifts his hand, inches away from me.

He says, "For what it's worth … what I saw in this dressing room tells me Cain was lucky while he had you."

I inhale a sharp gasp. "Asshole."

My fist cracks against his cheek.

He stumbles backward, hissing out the pain. "Damn, woman! You hit like Hunter."

I grind my teeth. I guess I like Hunter again. I'm fifty percent sure that Lutz was talking trash when he implied that Hunter and Cain are together, but if Hunter has put Lutz in his place, then I have to respect her.

Lutz says, "Thank you. I needed that. The pain helps take my mind off doing things I don't want to do."

I swallow my own pain and now my confusion. Did he deliberately provoke me just now? "You don't want to take me back to Boston."

He shakes his head. "I really don't."

With that, his hand snakes out and wraps around my arm. When I don't resist, he propels me to the dressing room door. Pulling it inward, he drives me directly toward a service door on the right, the opposite direction to the front of the shop.

I side-eye him. "You're not in protective gear today. That was a mistake."

"I don't make mistakes."

I smile. "Apparently you do."

My confident response makes him frown.

I prompt, "I'm told that collateral damage is unacceptable."

He stiffens a little. He stops pushing me. "So?"

"You don't want Parker to get hurt."

I tug left, swinging around to reveal the woman in question, her feet planted in the middle of the dressing room corridor, holding two dresses that she promptly throws on the ground.

I love the fact that she moves so quietly; Lutz didn't hear her approach.

Storm clouds gather across Parker's expression, her lips compress, and a deep frown mars her forehead.

Lutz slowly releases me, unclasping his hand from my arm. He takes a careful step away from me.

"*You.*" Parker walks straight up to him and pokes him in the chest. "Stay away from Grace."

Despite the force behind her movement, she barely makes an impact. Lutz stares at her finger as if it's a feather. But his frown disappears, lifting.

His expression changes, becomes intent, his head tilting, the slightest challenge entering his eyes. It's the same way Cain looks at me. As if he's daring me to make a move...

Lutz whisks Parker's hand into his, capturing her fingertips within his palm, making her gasp. He carefully draws her hand up to his lips and brushes a kiss across her knuckles, never taking his eyes from hers.

Her focus shifts to his wounded lip.

"Oh," she says, her eyes widening. "You're hurt."

The hole in my heart widens. Parker can't fight her inner nature; she can't stop caring, even about this man who could kill her in a heartbeat. I can never see the world the way she does, as if everyone is innately capable of goodness. I need her in my life, but I can't have that either.

Lutz gives her a crooked grin. "It's all better now."

Then he releases her and spins to me with a ferocious glare. "Remember who you're putting in danger."

Parker. She's in danger every second she spends with me.

He strides toward the service door, but I call after him. "Not for long, Lutz Logan."

He half-turns with a frown, an imposing force paused in the doorway.

I say, "You'll see me again soon. At a time of my choosing."

His frown clears. A hint of respect enters his eyes. "I'll be waiting."

I give him a nod. I will go with him, but only as far as it takes to lead my enemies away from Parker and Cain. After that, I'll disappear again.

Parker rubs her hand where Lutz kissed it, blinking away her surprise. "Assassins are very confusing."

I sigh, coming back to myself. "Men are confusing."

She says, "Not Cain."

I laugh. "Especially Cain."

Parker says, "It's hard for me to reconcile *what* Cain is with *who* he is."

I take her arm, needing her to hear me. "He's still your brother. He hasn't changed."

"But there's darkness in him that I never knew about."

"We all have darkness. Cain channels it in a way that balances out the scales of justice."

She searches my eyes. "Do you truly believe that?"

"I have to. Or else I'd run screaming from the lot of them." *Which I'm going to do. Just without the screaming part.*

She gives me a small smile. "I guess."

I say, "He needs you to forgive him, Parker."

She chews on her lip before focusing on me again. "I think you should get that dress. It matches your eyes."

I glance in the far mirror. The dress matches the

color of my contact lenses. Only the deepest violet would match my eyes.

I see Parker safely home, where I quietly alert Sarah that it's too dangerous for me to visit the apartment again. She gives me a sad nod and then Spencer drives me back to the Realm.

Cain waits for me, leaning against the doorway into the Realm, a smile growing on his face when he sees the bags I'm carrying.

I miss a step. That smile. It makes my heart squeeze painfully inside my chest. I'd give anything to have a lifetime of Cain's smiles, but now I have to build distance between us. Somehow, I have to honor my promise to tell him I'm leaving, and then I have to make myself go.

Before I can speak, he says, "I'm glad you're back. It wasn't the same without you."

No ... he can't say that to me right now.

I search for the coldness in my heart, trying to numb myself, needing a protective cloak around emotions. All I find is anger. *Damn Lutz Logan. Damn Lady Tirelli. And damn Slade Baines.*

I growl, "I hope you're prepared for how expensive this dress was, Cain Carter."

He doesn't miss anything, certainly not the heat in my response.

His voice lowers, slightly cautious. "Consider it a gift."

"In exchange for what?" Too sharp. I try to swallow it back. My emotions are getting the better of me, but I can't rein them in. "Gifts come with strings."

Oh, if only I could hate Cain, too.

I try to take a calming breath. But all I can think about is my warm toes and his deep breathing in the morning. *Why did this have to be so hard?*

A mask falls over his face as he carefully takes my arm, giving me entrance to the Realm. "Not this gift."

"Why not?" I spin to face him as soon as I step foot on the Realm's pebbled courtyard. "Why are you doing any of this?"

He contemplates me for a moment, searching my eyes the same way that Parker did earlier. Can he read my thoughts? Is that an assassin's skill?

He draws nearer to me, his voice lowering. "What happened out there?"

"I ran into Lutz." Having answered his question, I rush on, "Is it true that Slade Baines is entitled to fight you?"

"Yes."

My eyes widen. I breathe, "Lutz was telling the truth."

Cain is like stone, his jaw like granite. He squares

his shoulders, his muscles flexing, and maybe for the first time since I met him ... I'm looking at an assassin.

It sends a chill through my heart.

He says, "Slade has given me the courtesy of waiting until I become Master."

"Wait ... *what?*" I gasp, but I want to scream. I drop the bags and stumble backward, wobbling over the edge of the pathway, the breath knocked out of me. "You've already arranged it? You're going to fight him?"

"Yes."

The world spins around me; panic billows up from my stomach. I'm going to throw up. Or scream. Or run. "Is he strong enough to kill you?"

Cain's response is simple, ringing with truth. "He is."

CHAPTER THIRTEEN

This isn't happening. It can't be...

Cain's determined eyes meet mine and my heart plummets, my emotions spiral; coherent thoughts stop.

My voice is strangled. "You never should have helped me."

He reaches for me, closing the gap again. "Archer, listen to me. Slade won't—"

The breath stops in my lungs. He called me *Archer...*

I dart backward, my hands shooting out, keeping him at a distance. I need to ask one more question, the most important one. "If I leave, will Slade stay away from you?"

"Yes, but—"

I spin for the door. I wanted to leave on my own terms. I thought I could stay another day, take a moment, say a proper goodbye. I have nothing with me, no belongings, no money, but it doesn't matter. This isn't how I wanted to go, but I can't stay another moment knowing that Cain is walking to his death because of me.

I'm five paces away from the door when the pathway blurs. My back suddenly burns. My body is no longer cold but … far too hot. My gaze shifts upward to the sky, as if I could reach into it and pull it to me. At the same time, copper light streams around me, an undeniable force.

Cain appears in front of me, far faster than I ever expected. Light streams around him like sunlight. It curls around my torso and legs, caressing me like a breeze as he blocks the doorway.

"Archer, stop."

I pull up sharp. My heart is beating far too fast. My shoulder blades feel like they're going to explode; the pain is hard to process.

I'm … panicking.

I never panic. Not even when Dad was killed. But now I have to move, I have to run, I need to escape my own body. I remember Briar telling me not to die because of her.

Now it's Cain who is going to die.

I cry, "You can't die because of me. I'm not worth it."

His eyes widen, then narrow, his jaw setting. "Not worth it?"

He closes the gap between us. The copper light curls around me, a tangible force. Before I can draw breath, he wraps his arms around me, one around my waist, the other sweeping up my back.

His head tilts to mine. "You are worth every second."

Our surroundings shift, golden light solidifying in a dome around us, creating a visual barrier that blocks out the rest of the Realm, the sky, the door. We are enclosed in our own private space created by magic that hums around and inside me, calling my senses. The world expands around me and the burn in my back eases.

My heart hammers hard in my chest as Cain searches my eyes. His nearness is intoxicating, his hand stroking the back of my neck, tangling in the strands of hair, his other palm flexing against the small of my back, making me arch.

I close my eyes against the tears I won't cry.

I gasp when his lips brush my cheek.

His question is soft. "What can I do to make you believe me?"

He plants a kiss on my other cheek. Then his lips

brush across my temple, trailing kisses down to my earlobe.

My heart rate begins to slow, to calm.

His thumb brushes slowly back and forth across my neck, cradling my head, and I shiver when he drops the lightest kiss against the corner of my lips.

"Archer?"

I open my eyes, needing to know: "Why did you stop calling me Grace?"

"Because I want you to know that I see you." He pauses, his lips mere inches from mine, his strong hands making me tingle. "I want you to know that you're real to me. You matter. *You*. Not your alias."

"Why?" It's the question I'm always asking him but he never answers.

He draws me even closer, his lower hand curving around my waist. "Why do you care if Slade kills me?"

"Because I…" My breathing spirals out of control again. The idea of Cain ever dying, of losing him, makes me want to rip apart the world. "Because you … because I want … because I need…"

"What do you want?"

I can't go without knowing what kissing him feels like. I lean forward and up, instinctive movements, rising just the slightest on my toes, my hands planted on his chest.

I press my lips against Cain's.

His are soft, parting slightly as he inhales against my mouth. Craving spreads through me, making me want to stay right there, making me want more, but with it comes terror. I kissed him. Not the other way around.

I draw apart, but he doesn't push me away, following me instead.

He tips his head to mine, whispering, "Finally."

His lips meet mine, soft at first, like a gentle question. My senses hum and I sigh against his mouth, melting into him, responding when he deepens the kiss, my hands sliding out between us to find the muscular curves of his back and shoulders, pulling him closer. The intensity of his kiss increases and his breathing hitches when I arch into him. My own is rapid, but not from panic. I can't get close enough. I tug on the back of his shirt, sliding my hands beneath it, needing to feel his bare skin under my hands while I kiss him. Just once.

Before I know it, he pulls me, still kissing me, two steps left so that his back is pressed against the side of the golden dome that he created around us. He lifts me up against him, one strong hand still cradling my head while his other strokes down my thigh, drawing my knee up so that it is propped against the wall next to his hip and my lower half presses against his. I gasp as intense need rises inside me, sensing him smile against my mouth.

The dome shifts, changes, around us, softening beneath my knee, lowering us both so that I can rest my other leg beside him. My senses kick into high gear, overwhelming sensation spiraling through me.

Cain's lips become demanding against mine, his hands finding their way beneath my shirt, his touch burning across my waist, both hands wrapping around my torso beneath my breasts, holding me in a way that makes me want so much more. I can't help but moan against his mouth, dragging his shirt upward so I can explore his chest and back. But ... dammit ... I have to stop kissing him if I want to take his shirt off, and if I stop kissing him...

Reality will come crashing back to me.

I don't want reality. I don't want to leave. I want to steal this moment and make it last forever.

As if he hears my thoughts, he whispers against my mouth, "Don't go."

I press my lips to his, capturing his next words, trying to keep them for myself.

"Stay with me," he says. "I'll fight any battle to have you in my life."

I hold his declaration close to my heart, but I whisper, "Not if it kills you. That would break my heart, Cain."

He releases my waist to brush the hair from my face, dropping kisses on my lips, maintaining contact, as he speaks. "Promise me you'll stay until I'm Master. Give me time to figure out a solution."

I groan with frustration. "It's not just Slade. Lady Tirelli will target you as long as I'm here. She got to my father, she can get to you."

He doesn't allow me to pull back, pressing kisses against the corner of my lips, trailing them across my cheeks before he captures my gaze. "Lady Tirelli was already targeting me. She knows about the assassin's world. She will continue to come after me—and Parker—even if you leave."

I search his eyes, wanting to believe him, wanting any excuse to stay.

A gentle smile breaks across his face. "I'm safer if you're watching my back—and Parker's. As you found out on the first day, I can't exactly count on my own people right now."

His kisses trail to my ear and down the side of my neck, making it difficult to focus. Or to think, for that matter. He could ask me anything right now and I would say "Yes." As his gaze flashes to mine for a moment, a dare glows in them, making me gasp.

"You were waiting for me to kiss you."

He nods, nuzzling the soft spot beneath my ear. "I wanted you to choose me. Not because you were stuck here. Or because I gave you a gift. Or because of coffee and muffins in the morning..."

I squeeze my eyes closed. "Cain, I—"

He suddenly draws back from me with a frown, head tilted, glancing across to my right. "Someone's calling me."

Pain shoots through me. "You have to go."

Instead of getting up, he kisses me, his hands stroking down my arms and back up to my shoulders. "We aren't done here, Archer."

His thumb brushes my cheek. "Promise me you'll give me another day to sort this out." His eyes meet mine. "I need you to stay." Then a glimmer of a smile grows on his lips, making me want to kiss them again. "I'll beg if I have to."

I chomp my lip. "Don't do that, Cain Carter." I press my cheek against his, soaking up the sensation of his strong jaw next to mine. "I'll stay. But the moment my presence here endangers you or Parker, I have to go."

His hands graze my waist. "Thank you."

He picks me up and places me on the ground. I hurry to tuck in my shirt and smooth my hair, but he grins at me, laughter on his lips. "Don't worry about your clothing. They know what we were doing in here."

My cheeks flame as his appreciative gaze runs the full length of me. But he is somber as he says, "Assassins don't have normal relationships. We might train in a pack, but after that ... we're alone."

His expression shifts, his assassin's face stern and

unforgiving as he turns his attention to the dome around us. With a simple wave of his hand, the shield around us disappears, revealing Brenna and two assassins waiting on the other side.

Brenna all but taps her foot. "Master, you have an urgent mission."

Cain's response is a single nod before he catches my eye. "Come with me, Grace."

Brenna scowls as she follows Cain to one of the nearby buildings—a low one that reminds me of a school administration office.

Two men are waiting in the room when we arrive. They are both tall, muscular, dark-haired, multiple tattoos decorating their arms. They wear threat like a cloak around their bodies. There are no windows in this room, but both men gleam at their edges as if they are backlit with sunlight. Their gazes glide across me, landing on Cain as he strides behind the desk in the center of the room.

I stand to the side of the room, shoving my bags against the wall and choosing the furthest position from Brenna.

The silence is deafening as Cain sizes up the visitors. I can't read anything in his expression while he wears the Master assassin's mask, but a shiver runs to my toes. I would never want to oppose him. If it's true that Slade could beat Cain, then I sure as hell never want to meet Slade.

Cain says to the men, "Why have you asked for me?"

The man on the right steps forward. "Our brother is being held hostage by a rival gang. The usual channels of justice … are not available to us."

I consider the men carefully. It sounds like a gang war … not something I would want to get involved in.

Cain's gaze narrows, his green eyes hard and glittering. "That wasn't my question."

The man swallows. "Our brother is being held by ten men, all heavily armed. You have killed as many as five on a mission. You are the only Horde assassin who has a chance to bring him back alive."

Cain unfolds his arms. His expression reveals nothing as he reaches for the large book on the table, turns it to face the men, and opens it. He holds out a pen.

The man who spoke lets out the breath he was holding, takes the pen, and swiftly writes in the book. I crane my neck to see what he's writing. It looks like names—ten of them—then a monetary amount, a mention about his brother, an address, and then the man signs his own name. He places the pen carefully in the middle of the book when he's done.

Cain swivels the book and countersigns.

He says, "You have written in my ledger, but it's the Guardian's choice whether to sanction the mission. Your brother's life is in her hands for now. If her writing glows golden, the mission is sanctioned. If blue, it is not."

When the word "Sanctioned" appears on the page in glowing golden script, I glance at the men, but I suddenly realize that nobody else is looking at the words except Cain. Their focus is on the glow above the pages. Brenna blinks at the glow and looks away, rubbing her forehead as if it gives her a headache.

Cain says to the men, "Now your brother's life is in my hands."

As soon as the visitors leave, Cain spins to Brenna and the other assassins. All he says is, "Weapons."

Brenna nods. "Ready in ten minutes." She spins on her heels and strides away with the other two assassins. Cain turns to the book as I reach his side, but I place my hand over his before he can close it.

The names on the page are like a deadly threat. "Ten."

He pauses beside me, his voice lowering. "It's not impossible."

I swing to him, taking his face in my hands, forcing him to look at me. "I don't like it, Cain. I don't like … them."

He searches my eyes. "What is it?"

I suddenly wish he would call me "Archer," because Archer is the fighter who knows when to trust her instincts. Archer knows how to shoot a gun. Grace reads books and inhales Cain's kisses like air she needs to breathe.

"They didn't look right."

"What do you mean?"

I chew my lip. "I see it sometimes, and I guess now I'm wondering if it's magic. People sometimes have this ... glow around them—it's like looking into sunlight. I always thought it was a trick of the light, but there are no windows in here."

He stares at me, his hands freezing on my shoulders. "You saw that?"

"What is it?"

"It's called an aura. All magical beings have them. Those men are wolf shifters: Gray Wolves. They're enemies of the Jaguars. Their turf war has been going on for decades. But ... you shouldn't be able to see their auras."

"Why not?"

"Humans can't. Only other magical beings can."

I swallow, try to smile. "But you can."

He lifts his hand. "I have this."

It's his assassin's ring.

I shuffle backward, drawing away from him, confusion swamping me. "I don't know..."

He studies me, suddenly cautious. "You see through blurs and you see auras... Can you do something for me, please, Grace? Tell me what this says?"

He points to the open ledger, his forefinger pressed next to the address on the page.

I stare at it. Then at him. I remember how nobody else looked at it. I read out the address in a rush. Then I say, "I'm not supposed to be able to read that, am I?"

He is frozen beside me. "Nobody can read a ledger except the client who writes in it and the assassin to whom it belongs. Everyone else sees squiggles."

"I don't ... have answers for you."

Fear is a deep pit in my stomach. I don't understand many things about myself. I don't understand why I'm calm when I hold a weapon, as if I'm channeling instincts I don't have access to at any other time. I don't understand why I check out afterward. I don't understand why I can see through blurs, and I sure as hell don't know why I can see auras.

Cain closes the gap, searching my face like he's digging for explanations and coming up empty-handed. "You're human. You don't have an aura. None at all."

I lay my hand on his arm, my concern for him overshadowing my confusion. "Let me come with you today. I don't know why I can read your ledger—or how I can see auras. But my instincts tell me you need backup."

He grimaces. "You're not wrong."

He moves to a cabinet at the side of the room, pulls open a drawer, and lifts out a wad of folders.

He places them on the table and opens them one by one. "Usually, the Guardian sends us all of the information she has on a target, but I don't have time to wait for it. In this case, I already know what I'm dealing with."

I can barely look at the images that confront me in each of the folders, all the victims, the violence, evidence in the form of statements and photographs, all of it attributed to the names in the ledger.

Cain says, "Jaguars don't usually gather in packs, but these guys have learned that there is strength in numbers. Each crime is worse than the last." His fists clench. "I've been waiting for someone to write their names in my ledger."

I spin to him, my fear for him escalating because of the evidence. "But not all at once. Is there any rule that says I can't help?"

He considers my question. "The Assassin's Code is very specific. The first rule is that assassins don't kill each other. To break that means death. But that isn't relevant here.

"The second rule is that all assassinations must be sanctioned by the Guardian. No problems there, either. The third rule is that collateral damage is unacceptable, but again, that only applies to me, not you. The only rule that affects you is the fifth. Which you already broke."

He smiles suddenly. "Just don't get between me and

someone I'm gunning for or you'll break the fifth again."

"I promise I won't." I give him a curious smile. "You skipped the fourth rule."

"A failed assassination can't be attempted again. That's why Briar is safe now."

I can't help my sudden spark of hope. "So ... if a Legion assassin tries to kill me and fails ... then I'll be safe?"

He shakes his head at me. "In your case, only Slade will try, and he ... he won't fail."

I sigh. "Are there any other rules I should know about?"

He is somber. "The sixth rule is that an assassin must not interfere in an assassination. By bringing you here ... I broke that rule. It's what gives Slade the right to fight me. But the seventh rule is what keeps him out of my territory: A Master may not enter another Faction's Realm without permission. The consequence is death."

"In other words, he has to wait for his pound of flesh?"

"It would be nice if that was the end of it, but the Guardian is our arbiter. She makes sure nobody breaks the rules. Which is why, if I don't stop interfering, she will sanction Slade to travel here."

I swallow. "Well, now that I'm schooled up on all

the rules, I think I can say with certainty that I won't break any of them by coming with you today."

"Okay, then." His gaze sweeps me in a way that gives me goosebumps.

He says, "Let's find you a protective suit."

CHAPTER FOURTEEN

*J*uliet arrives at Cain's quarters carrying multiple suits in different sizes for me to try on.

Cain gives me a brief smile after he ushers her inside. "I adjusted the shields to let her through."

Juliet is wide-eyed as she glances around the room. She attempts to splay her arms while juggling the clothing. "It's an honor, Master."

Cain hides a smile and heads to the master bedroom to get ready, closing the door behind him.

I turn back to Juliet. "I take it Novices never visit the Master's quarters."

"We aren't allowed inside the Cathedral until we become Superiors. I don't know why the Master made an exception."

I consider her. "Because I trust you. And Cain trusts me."

She clears her throat, turning to business. "You should try these on for size. The suit needs to fit you like a glove or it won't protect you. I can help you pull it on."

I remove my jeans and t-shirt in the living area, allowing her to help me shimmy into the first suit—too big. But the next one fits much better. She shows me how to do up the hidden clasps at the side. Then she asks if she can braid my hair.

I check myself in the mirror when we're done. My hair is tied back in tight braids, leading into a single braid that rests across my shoulder. I'm amazed at the effect the suit has on my appearance. All my curves and muscles are suddenly emphasized—more feminine, but also more dangerous. We even have gloves so we don't leave fingerprints.

Juliet gives me a broad smile. "You should be an assassin."

I hide my smile. "Hmm."

Cain appears in the doorway, dressed in his own suit, the dark material hugging every powerful muscle, his height and strength accentuated, his eyes glittering. His personal daggers disappear into holsters he wears around his body. There are many empty spots for more. An appreciative smile grows on his face as he looks me over.

He says, "Thank you, Juliet. Don't tell anyone about this, please."

"I understand." She leans in to me before she disappears. "Give them hell, Mistress."

The door closes behind her.

Cain says, "Brenna will have the weapons waiting in the entrance, but she can't know you're coming with me. We'll leave through the exit on the other side of the Realm. You need to stay out of sight until then."

"I will." I follow him outside and down the stairs, walking at a prowl.

When we reach the lowest level, he places his hand on my arm, signaling for me to stay put.

Voices reach us from the entranceway.

Brenna demands, "What are you doing here, Novice?"

Juliet's reply is confident. "The Master requested my presence."

"I know that already or you would be a pile of ash. Answer my question!"

There's a pause. I picture Juliet rising up to her full five foot four inches. "If he has chosen not to share his plans with you, then it's not my place to speak."

"Insolent!"

Slap.

My eyes widen. Cain shakes his head at me, a finger raised, mouthing: *Wait.*

Juliet's voice is filled with threat. "You will not touch me again, Superior."

Brenna hisses, "I'll hit you as much as I want, runt."

Thud.

Thud-thud.

Then silence. I need to get out there. I won't allow Juliet to be bullied by that bitch.

Cain reads my mind. He gestures sternly for me to stay where I am as he strides around the corner.

I risk a glance, my eyes widening at what I see.

The two male assassins lie on the ground. Both are out cold. Brenna's face is planted on the floor while Juliet wrenches her arm backward, using a knee to pin Brenna down. Juliet quickly follows through with a hit to Brenna's face, knocking her out.

She drops Brenna's arm and stands to attention as Cain approaches. "Master."

He gives her a nod. "Juliet."

Juliet stands guard over the prone assassins while Cain opens the trunk that sits at the side of the corridor. He pulls out guns and daggers, which he holsters around his body. Then he produces another holster, a smaller one, into which he slips extra daggers and guns. He brings that one to me, fitting it securely around my body, his hands resting on my sides when he's done.

"One more thing..." He heads back to the box and returns with two semi-automatic machine guns.

In the distance, Juliet spins on her heels, leaving Brenna and her guys on the floor while Cain and I disappear out the back entrance before they revive.

The door opens into a hanger containing two helicopters and multiple SUVs and motorcycles. We take one of the SUVs, an innocuous-looking one with tinted windows.

Cain surprises me by driving like a demon through the streets of Austin. He side-eyes me at one point, saying, "This is why I have drivers. I should have warned you not to get in a vehicle with me behind the wheel."

I let out a laugh, clutching the seat. "I can't drive, so I'm not judging."

He looks surprised. "Nobody taught you?"

"Dad died when I was sixteen, so I never learned."

He says, "I'll have to do something about that."

I reply only with, "Hmm."

He laughs, takes the next turn at speed, and tips his head. "Maybe Spencer would be a better teacher…"

We head north, twenty-five minutes out of the city, and up into the hills, traveling away from the suburbs into a secluded area. The view is breathtaking, but I'm not here to enjoy it.

Cain slows the vehicle and pulls off the road, parking it beneath a spreading tree. He says, "The house is well guarded, but the security guys are not my targets, which is why I carry this." He points to one of the larger firearms. "Tranquilizer gun. Once we take them out, we'll need to gain access to the home. The hostage will be in a cage. If we're lucky, he'll be on display. That's the way the Jaguars usually roll."

An unexpected thrill shoots through me. I've read enough books to imagine what a shifter looks like in animal form, but I'm not sure how different the reality will be from the fantasy. "Will they shift?"

"If threatened. They're stronger in animal form." He grins at me, but his smile fades. "They have very powerful jaws. Don't assume they can't get through the suit."

Exiting the vehicle, I collect the weapons I had to remove to sit comfortably.

Cain says, "We walk from here. Hold my hand and I'll blur you."

His strong palm covers mine, his ring glows, and a force passes through me. I shiver, goosebumps rising on my skin as our surroundings change. My environment is suddenly unfocused, as if I'm looking at it through a sheet of water.

"Nobody can see or hear us inside the blur."

I try to catch my breath. My whole body tingles. I should be afraid, but I'm not. In fact, I feel the opposite. My senses thrum, every part of my heart and mind is alive, including that old burn in my shoulders. But so far it doesn't hurt. I roll my shoulders without breaking contact with Cain as we finally approach a large gate at the entrance to a long driveway.

Two men guard the gate, both armed.

I say, "No security cameras. Unlike your place."

Cain grunts. "I have infrared so I can detect someone who is blurred. Blurring makes us undetectable to sight, sound, and smell, but it doesn't obscure our body heat from infrared."

He transfers my hand to his waist to keep me invisible before he relaxes into a perfect shooting position and takes aim. His movements are a blur as he takes two quick, clean shots. The men snatch at the darts in their shoulders, wobbling before they drop to the pavement.

Cain drags them off the road. "We have an hour before they come to."

Inside the compound, Cain tranquilizes three more guards on the grounds, and two at the door before we hustle inside. "It won't be long before those guys are missed. We have to hurry."

He gestures left to the living area from which most of the noise is coming.

It's filled with tacky furniture; most of the chairs are covered in furs. I don't want to look too closely, since they could be trophies from the gang war between the shifters. True to Cain's prediction, a cage sits at the side of the room with a clear space around it. It looks like part of the furniture, a place that is often used. A man of the same physique as the men who requested the mission paces back and forth inside the cage.

I count ten men either lounging or drinking at various spots within the room. Four sit at the table to the far left playing cards. Four more recline on the leather couches; two stand on either side of the cage, loosely guarding it. One of the guards goads the hostage, splashing his beer into the cage, snarling, "We'll spill your blood soon, wolf."

Cain is quiet beside me, his gaze shifting from one to the other before he says, "These are the ten. All of their deaths are sanctioned. The only possible collateral is the hostage."

He gestures to the cage, then at the men playing cards at the table furthest from it. "We should take out those four, then become visible so the others shoot at us and not in the hostage's direction. Can you take out those two—?"

I bump my hip against his to maintain contact, and take aim with the semi-automatic at the two men furthest to the left.

Cain gives me a smile of appreciation. "Yes, you can."

He lifts his own weapon, taking position. "I'll move away from you as soon as those four are dead. Are you ready?"

I return his smile. I've been calm for the last hour.

I'm holding more weapons than I ever have before and covered in protective material that resists bullets and daggers. I've never been more ready.

I guess I'll soon find out if the suit repels jaws, too.

As soon as Cain fires, I follow, pulling off two quick lethal shots before ducking and rolling, coming up on one knee and shooting two of the shifters on the couch as well. Six down already. Cain flashes me a look of surprise, but his focus quickly returns to the battle. The remaining four will not be so easy.

They dive behind separate lounge chairs, weapons in hand, returning fire.

I cover Cain as he darts between a stream of bullets, targeting the single male shooting from behind the nearest armchair. Cain powers up to it, stepping from the seat to the back, his weight toppling the chair so that the guy has no choice but to dart out from behind it. He slams right into Cain's boot and meets a quick bullet.

Cain stands between the remaining men and the hostage, who dove to the back of the cage as soon as the fighting started. I remain on the other side of the room, covering the exit on this side.

The return gunfire stops and growls meet my ears. I shudder at the sharp sounds. Three big cats slink from behind the furniture, their golden pelts flecked with inky black swirls. They are beautifully savage, their eyes lustrous. Perfect killers.

A bit like me.

Cain immediately swaps one of his guns for a dagger. I maintain both my pistols. The minute the jaguars leap, the game will change.

Instinctively, I duck, roll, and drop to the floor seconds before the nearest beast launches off the ground. I empty a clip into its belly as it flies over me, its attack mistimed, a deadly mistake. With a dying yowl, it hits the floor and slides across the rug. I twist, both weapons pointed at the other two jaguars, but they're too close to Cain now.

Their claws are a vicious blur as they leap at him, knocking him against the wall. His gun goes off twice before it clicks empty. One of the jaguars twists away from him, landing on the floor with a thud, mortally wounded. But the other knocks Cain's dagger out of his hand, catching his shoulder between its powerful jaws.

Cain said that jaguars could get through our suits, and the beast's hold is only inches above Cain's heart. The creature shakes its head, savaging at Cain's shoulder, forcing him down into a half-kneeling position. It slashes with its claws, brutal cuts that would tear his torso apart if not for the suit. Cain's harness is a casualty of the beast's assault, falling to the floor with a clatter.

I hesitate, both my guns aimed at the jaguar. I can't risk shooting Cain.

Cain roars, desperately trying to reach his weapons as the jaguar continues to maul at his shoulder. Giving up, he slaps his hand against the beast's muzzle. Golden light streams around his hand, telling me he is harnessing his assassin's magic instead.

I race to another position, prepare to take aim, then freeze.

Blood splatters the wall behind Cain, a crimson splash. I can't tell if it's Cain's or the jaguar's. My heart stops when Cain falters and his magic fades.

"No!" I don't think. I cast my guns aside, leverage off the nearest couch, and propel myself onto the jaguar's back, my hands clamping around each of its jaws.

Its teeth are hot and slippery, its muzzle hard and bristly.

With a scream, I pull the jaguar's jaws apart, releasing Cain's shoulder, the force of my movement propelling the beast and me backward. It falls with me, trying to twist to right itself, landing heavily on my torso and legs, one of its claws raking down my side.

As we fall, I pull my arms apart with all my strength.

Crack.

The sickening crunch washes over me as I rip its jaws off. Blood sprays across my body and my neck, and the beast's dying roar fills the room before it stops struggling.

I lie beneath it, pressed into the floor, my breathing rapid. Far too rapid. I need to get to Cain, make sure he's okay, but when I try to push the dead jaguar off myself, fire rips through my back, a scorching burn inside my shoulder blades, making me writhe.

I'm not holding any weapons, and now … now the consequences of fighting will annihilate me…

"Archer!"

The sound of thudding feet reaches me before Cain's face appears above me. He is pale. I can't see his shoulder from this angle, but he's alive. I breathe out my relief even though pain floods me. The fire in my back is trying to push me upward. I need to stand. After that, I'm not sure, but I can't lie here anymore.

I try to speak, but … another shadow casts over me.

A scream rises to my throat. "Cain!"

A brick swings against Cain's head, cracking into him.

He drops to the floor, his face turned in my direction. Blood trickles from a wound in his forehead, but the rise and fall of his chest tells me it isn't mortal.

Two faces appear above me. It's the two men who asked for the mission. One of them breaks off, and within moments the cage clangs and the third man is free to hover over me too. He licks his lips at me in a way that makes me shudder.

My left hand inches across the floor, finding cold steel. I whip the gun upward and pull the trigger.

Empty clicks echo over … and over…

"You're all out of bullets, darlin'." The man who wrote in the ledger tilts his head at me, his aura glowing dangerously before he slams a fist into my face.

Oomph. My head hits the side of the floor, the world spins. I'm pretty sure I'm bleeding, but I glare up at him.

He looks a little surprised. I guess he expected to knock me out. It takes more than a single hit to do that. The pain of the assault is nothing compared to the force in my spine, and it only makes me mad. I need to get up. I struggle to move the jaguar, but it weighs a ton. I can't shift it.

The former hostage's aura glow dangerously, a gray glimmer around his silhouette as he says, "She's a pretty thing, isn't she, Jared?"

The man who hit me growls, "She's our ticket to power, Adrian. Lady Tirelli wanted us to kill Cain. If we take this woman back to her too, she'll make us kings."

I growl up at them. "This was a trap."

Jared smiles at me. "Yes and no. Adrian really was a hostage, so we asked the good Lady for help. She said she had a better plan: get Cain to do our dirty work for us, then we kill him. If we do that, she promised to give us control of the city. But ... if we take *you* to her, she will make us her sons."

The third man hangs back while the former hostage, Adrian, snarls, "I spent three days in that stinking cage. I can have fun first, right?"

Jared smiles. "As long as she's in one piece, I don't see why not."

I try to blink through my tears. I'm not afraid, not of them. I'm not crying because of their threats.

The pain in my shoulder blades spreads down my spine, throbbing through me in sickening waves. It is only getting worse, and any second now I'm going to start screaming. I need a new weapon, anything to make the agony stop.

I whimper, casting a desperate gaze around the room for the nearest gun, my sobs making the men snicker.

Relief floods me when Cain's fallen dagger glints at the corner of my vision, inches away from me on the bloody carpet. I creep my hand toward it, trying to move without drawing attention. *Damn!* It's too far away. But the three men are about to free me to have their fun. I struggle to take deep breaths—I just have to wait another moment until they release me.

They grab hold of the jaguar, huffing and pulling together. The beast's fur drags across me in the opposite direction to the dagger. The jaguar's weight lifts. Nearly enough...

I'll be free in two seconds. Two seconds until I can grab the dagger. Then the pain will stop and I will be okay again...

A flicker of movement catches my eye. Cain's eyelids squint open, widening as he focuses on me. His gaze flicks to the men and then to the weapon I'm reaching for. Alarm shoots across his face.

The jaguar's weight lifts. *Finally!*

I slip, roll, and lunge for the dagger, hand outstretched, wrapping my fingers around it.

At the same time, Cain shouts, "Archer, no! Don't touch it!"

The startled men fall back as the dagger whips out of my hand, rising into the air all on its own. I scream as it shoots directly at my face.

I scramble backward, trying to avoid the blade as it forces me across the room, jabbing directly at my right eye as I jump and run from it.

The men's laughter follows me until I thud into the wall. The dagger stops, poised at my eye level, its tip ready to impale me. It stops just in time. I try to move, but it follows me side to side, so close to my eye that I'm pinned and can't move either way.

"Archer!" Cain jumps to his feet, shakes himself as if he's fighting concussion, and launches at the two nearest men, power streaming around his body.

Jared and his brother fight back, but Adrian darts away, racing toward me, a gleam in his eyes. Wolf's eyes. The animal inside him shimmers in every angle of his face, his white teeth, his vicious grin.

He jerks to a halt in front of me. "Aww, pretty thing. You're in a spot of trouble now, aren't you?"

He doesn't try to take Cain's dagger—he's smart enough to steer clear of it. Instead he produces his own, running it over my body, starting at my knee and drawing it up my thigh, humming to himself as the tip travels all the way up to my face. He positions it at the base of my chin above my suit's neckline, pointing the dagger toward my spine.

If I shift, I'll impale myself on Cain's dagger.

If I don't move, the wolf shifter will stab me through the throat.

I have nowhere to run.

CHAPTER FIFTEEN

*a*drian snarls, "Your Master will decide your fate now." He shouts over his shoulder: "Assassin! Give yourself up or I will kill your woman!"

Cain releases Jared from a throat hold and stays his boot from cracking the ribs of the other shifter, allowing them to scramble away from him.

My vision blurs. The pain in my back is too much, beyond endurance. I risk impaling my eye as I hunch my shoulders forward, flexing against the dagger at my throat, trying to find relief. I cut myself on it. Blood runs down my neck, making the shifter twitch.

Cain's response is a roar, but I barely hear it through my pain. "If you hurt her, I will break the Code and kill you all."

The force inside me is tearing me apart. It's like a tornado swirling inside my chest that has nowhere to go but to consume every part of me. I squeeze my eyes closed as the pain shreds my mind into pieces, my thoughts split apart, and only instinct remains.

I can't move my head or my neck, but I can use my arms, and Adrian is too arrogant to stand clear of me.

I growl, "Cain isn't my Master."

I kick Adrian hard in the groin. It's difficult to get leverage with my back pressed flat against the wall, but it's enough to force him backward, at which point I snatch his dagger out of his hands with my left hand, swinging it away from him. I hold on to the weapon, brandishing it as high as I can near my face, the handle pointed in his direction. I need him to try to take it back.

True enough, he comes back at me, snarling, arm swinging. I judge his balance, his gait, the angle of his fist ... I slam my right hand against his oncoming arm, deflecting the blow and knocking it sideways.

At the last moment, his fist bumps against Cain's dagger.

The dagger swings and zips toward Adrian with vicious jabs.

I'm free.

Quiet and cold, I flip Adrian's dagger into my right hand and fling it straight into his neck, its impact adding to the momentum of his backward scramble. He bumps into the nearest couch, sinking to a sitting position, a last rasp dragging out of his lungs.

Jared and the other man lurch in my direction, shouting for their brother, but Cain grabs both of them, yanking them backward, slamming them onto the floor.

He roars at them, "Nobody threatens my woman."

They scramble away from him, scooting on their backsides.

Jared screams, "You can't kill us. Our deaths aren't sanctioned. It's against your Code."

He's groveling, but behind his back he carefully pulls a handgun from the back of his jeans. He didn't kill Cain before and no doubt he wants to correct his mistake.

The force inside my body has progressed beyond painful.

My mind is numb. All I have is movement.

I run toward Adrian, yank his dagger out of his throat without touching Cain's, race across the rug, leap over the dead jaguar that fell on me, and fling the dagger into Jared's chest. As I race past him, I kick the dagger further into his chest, knocking him backward.

The other man—the one whose name I don't know—fires at me from his seat on the floor beside Jared, but the bullet sails wide. He shouts as I kick his firearm out, spin, grab his head, and twist.

He drops to the floor beside his brother.

My chest heaves; my entire body is on fire, but it's a cold burn, like being encased in ice.

Before I can turn to Cain, a flicker of light makes me stop. A single flame rises from each of the shifter's bodies, each flame a self-contained orb. My instincts kick in, my hands shoot out, and I catch one in each fist. The flames scorch my palms, searing me. Inside the flames, I sense ... a million moments in time, thousands of decisions, actions, all the pieces of these men's lives.

My eyes widen. I'm holding their souls.

They are dark and twisted. Bloody. Uncompromising death and violence fills my mind as I squeeze my fingers and crush the flames in my fists until my palms grow cold again, snuffing out their existence. When I open my fingers, expecting to see dust, there is nothing left. Nothing of those dark souls that I plucked from the air.

Inside I'm screaming, but when I turn to Cain I say, "You couldn't kill them. But I could."

He breathes, *"Damn. Archer."*

I take a step toward him. "It hurts, Cain."

He reaches for me, carefully pulling me into his arms. His warmth is like the sun; his assassin's magic is a balm on my wounded back, my shattered heart. With his warmth, and the power humming through him that speaks to my soul, the pain recedes. Feeling floods back into my arms and legs and all my pieces pull together again. I breathe out the cold inside me, not daring to open my eyes or move. I killed nine men

—six jaguars and three wolves. I don't know what happens now or how to deal with all the death around me.

Cain presses his cheek to my forehead, his voice muffled against my hair. "We need to get out of here."

I shudder, but I remember his shoulder and forehead, and reach up to check him over. His suit is torn at the shoulder, but the teeth marks are mere scratches.

He explains, "Its jaw snagged on the material."

"Then the blood I saw was the jaguar's? What about your head?"

He winces. "I have a headache. How does it look?"

"You need stitches. I can do them but they'll scar. I think you should call Sarah—"

He gives a vehement shake of his head. "If I call Sarah, Parker will hear about it. It's the last thing I want."

I frown, but there's no arguing with him on that. "Okay, but what about driving?"

"I'll take it slow."

I'm not convinced. I eye him as he hurries around the room, retrieving his daggers but leaving the other weapons.

The final dagger still hovers over the dead shifter's face. Cain plucks it from the air and it disappears into a holster.

When he returns to me, I ask, "Why did it attack me?"

"I have a spell cast over my daggers so that nobody else can touch them. The magic was woven by a very powerful witch, who warned me ... well ... she *tried* to warn me that I might regret it."

He swallows. "It almost cost your life."

He takes my hand and pulls me away from the room. I'm glad to leave it behind, along with the house.

When we return to the vehicle, several new SUVs arrive, but Cain waves them along. "It's the clean-up crew. They'll make sure the guards don't cause any trouble when they wake up."

True to his word, Cain keeps to the speed limit on the way back, but the silence stretches between us. I'm not sure how to fill it. All I keep coming back to is that my reputation—Archer Ryan's reputation—is not undeserved. I've killed a lot of people, but nobody who didn't threaten me or someone I cared about. Still ... there was a moment when Cain subdued Jared and his brother, when he beat them instead of killing them, that told me Cain was going to let them live. Not because of the Code, but because he isn't a killer at heart ... like I am.

Tears burn my eyes for the second time today. I can't help but wonder if I would be a completely different person if I were born into a different family, not into the underground with a father who made violence normal.

Or if I would be the same no matter who raised me.

We enter the Realm from the hanger and Cain ushers me inside the Cathedral and up to his quarters without encountering anyone. Once there, he is all business, giving me an icepack for my head where Jared thumped me. He gets one for himself before he retrieves a medical kit, sits on the couch, pats the coffee table opposite for me to sit on, and hands me a sterilized packet containing a needle.

I set to work, but I should have known that he would tackle the hard truths once I was a captive audience.

He says, "I understand now why you fight with impact. You kill with impact, too."

I focus on his forehead, trying to avoid facing the searching expression in his eyes. "I am Archer Ryan."

The depth in his response is unsettling. "You're more than that."

My hands tremble. What I saw at the shifter's house, holding their souls, I don't know whether Cain saw it too. I don't think he did. But I can't get it out of my head. Especially not the feeling that flooded me when I held their souls—the power that flooded through me—a power that felt so natural to me.

Cain confirms my thoughts when he asks, "What

were you doing at the end when you stood over them?"

Fear claws up from my stomach, but I can't lie to him. If only I could. "I crushed their souls."

He pauses for a beat. More than a beat.

He falls silent.

When I finish stitching him and I'm packing up the implements, he asks, "Archer ... may I see your back?"

I freeze with crippling fear, completely vulnerable, not wanting answers even though I need them. But I trust Cain. For the first time in my life, I actually trust someone.

I turn and unclasp the suit, peeling it off my arms and down to my waist, exposing my back.

Cain's presence is a powerful force behind me. His hands are warm and soothing against my tortured muscles, stroking across my shoulder blades and down my spine.

He whispers, "Copper ... I should have realized sooner..."

I close my eyes, tears burning behind them. I have to ask the question I'm afraid to ask. The question for which I don't want the answer.

Somehow, I form sound: "I'm not completely human, am I?"

He whispers, "You're not."

CHAPTER SIXTEEN

I try to swallow my fear. "What am I?"

He turns me to face him. "Something incredibly precious and rare. More dangerous than anyone else. You are … the perfect killer, but also, the perfect protector."

His big hands rest around my waist. "Will you wait here while I get something from the study?"

I nod and sink down to the couch, but when he leaves the room I twist, trying to see my shoulders, wanting to see what he sees, to know what he knows.

He returns with a book, which he opens to a wide illustration that stretches across both pages. He places it in my lap. Inside the picture, winged women battle each other in the air, their swords bloody, their expressions hard as stone, brilliant wings glinting in the overly bright sunlight. Beneath them, humans fight each other on a barren Earth littered with bodies.

Cain takes a seat beside me, pointing to one of the women. Her wings are gorgeous rose-gold, metallic in appearance, not feathery.

He says, "The women with copper wings are called Keres. They are the sworn enemy of the Valkyrie, whose wings are silver. Both races have the power to decide who lives and dies in battle. They can kill at will. Here, they are fighting for the right to claim the souls of the humans at war on Earth. Neither the Keres nor the Valkyrie has an aura, which makes them impossible to identify. They are the perfect assassins."

I protest, "But you said all magical beings have an aura."

"Not these women. What's more, they can only be killed in one of two ways..."

I lick my suddenly dry lips. "How?"

"By each other. Or by choosing to die." His serious gaze shifts from my eyes to my lips and back again. "They're also supposed to be extinct. Which is why ... to find you is ... incredible..."

I try to find my voice. "I don't have wings."

"I think you do. I think that's why you're in so much pain when you fight. You're trying to access your power, but it's locked up inside you for some reason. Your wings can't get out."

"How? And why now? I've never had this pain in my shoulders before."

He swallows, clears his throat. "I think it's because I brought you here. This Realm is made of assassin's magic. I think the magic triggered your wings."

"What about the way I collapse after a fight?"

"I think you connect with your power when you fight, but it's too much for your body to process."

I run my fingers over the image, the battle. "They all killed each other."

"That's the story."

"Why?"

He shakes his head. "I don't know."

"If I'm one of them … that means I'm alone."

"No." His response is vehement. He drops to his knees in front of me, searching my eyes. "You aren't alone. Not anymore."

Damn. He's going to break my heart.

I whisper, "I'm not your woman, Cain."

His gaze drops to my hands held in his. He is quiet, the stillness around him nearly absolute.

His lips part, but before he can speak, my fingers close around his.

I say, "But I could be."

I stop breathing, my words echoing back at me, spoken out of instinct, emotion, not logical thought, not rational. Reckless. I told Lutz Logan that I wouldn't stay with Cain, that I would give myself up. I have to go back to Boston with him. If what Cain said about me being Keres is true, then I don't have to be afraid of Slade. He can't kill me. Nothing can.

If it's true.

But maybe … maybe for tonight I can have something that I want, something good. I force myself to breathe, deeply and shuddering, afraid that I look as terrified as I feel.

The slow smile that breaks across Cain's face banishes my doubts and fears.

"Okay, then." He draws himself up to a standing position, pulling me with him. One hand closes over mine, but not tightly. The other tucks my hair behind my ear. "Let's clean off the battle."

I grimace. I haven't looked at myself in the mirror, but I can't be a pretty sight right now. Blood splattered on my neck and in my hair during the fight. My suit is pulled to my waist, and a glance tells me that all the gore is visible across my chest.

I shudder. "Right away, please."

He draws me through the bedroom, past the bed and into the bathroom, where he turns the shower on full, testing the temperature.

I wait in the middle of the room, uncertain, until he turns back to me with a question on his lips, the sudden heat in his eyes taking my breath away.

Cain has given me choices at every step. Right from the moment I bumped into him until now. This might be the most important choice, but it's mine to make. If it's a mistake, it's not one I'm going to regret.

I peel off the protective suit where I stand, leaving me in my underwear, but before I close the gap between us, I say, "I have to show you something."

With my heart in my throat, I veer toward the sink, pull open the drawer I've been using to store my things, and retrieve my contact lens case. Keeping my eyes down and avoiding the mirror, I remove my contacts, carefully clean them, and place them in the case.

Holding my breath, I raise my eyes to Cain and brace for his reaction.

His lips part. He becomes still. I wait for him to draw a breath.

When he does, it's an explosion of movement. He inhales at the same time as he moves, crossing the distance in three powerful strides, pulling me into his arms, one hand cradling my head, the other drawing my lower half close to his. Heat explodes through me at his nearness and I respond by arching closer to him, lifting my lips to his.

His mouth stops tantalizingly close to mine. His voice is a deep whisper: "Let me into your heart, Archer. You already have mine."

I want to. God help me, I need to.

"Yes." I run my hands into his dark hair, drawing him to me, pressing my lips to his. His mouth is warm on mine, his kiss gentle, his lips brushing my upper lip, my lower lip, then finally...

He draws me up and claims my mouth, the intensity in his kiss making me burn. I reach for the side of his suit, attempting to undo the clasps without breaking our kiss.

Impossible.

He smiles against my mouth and helps me pull it off. I catch a breath, my heart stuttering at his powerful form, perfect biceps, powerful thighs, and a chest that makes my stomach flip-flop. He pulls me back into his arms and draws me to the shower and under the stream of water. Warmth washes down my front and back. I tip my head back into it while Cain brushes my hair back, following the water flowing down my spine, his hands lingering across my lower back and the top of my underwear.

I gasp when I realize we're both still partially dressed.

Cain grins at my questioning look, arching an eyebrow at me. "That can wait."

Steam wafts around us as he soaks a cloth in water and draws it across my chin and neck, paying close attention to cleaning beneath my ears and across my left shoulder. I close my eyes, soaking up every touch, the graze of his thumbs, the soft swish of cloth, the brief pressure of his hands on my shoulders, my face, and finally the graze of his thumb over my lower lip.

I open my eyes to find him smiling at me.

He plants a slow kiss on my lips. Then he lathers up shampoo and massages it through my hair, washing out the battle.

"Close your eyes." He draws me into the water, drawing it through my hair to rinse it without getting suds in my eyes, kissing me again, our lips connected in the stream, before he shifts me out of it again.

Biting my lip, I hold out my hand for the cloth. When he gives it to me, I draw it across his chest and shoulder where his suit was ripped, trying to focus on cleaning him the same way he cleaned me, determined not to get distracted by the way his muscles shift beneath my hands, the slow smile lingering on his lips, or the way his breath catches when my cleaning efforts morph into an exploration of his chest, my fingertips sliding over his shoulders, down his arms, drawing myself closer.

The cloth slips out of my fingers.

He reaches back to turn off the water, taking my hand in his. Outside the shower, he wraps an oversized towel around my shoulders, pulling it all the way around himself, binding us together inside it.

My body aches. I am so close to him but I want to be closer. I tip my head up to see him. Before I can speak, he nuzzles his cheek against mine, dropping light kisses on my neck, chin, the corner of my mouth, then down my neck to my shoulder. He carefully pries my damp bra strap off my shoulder, kissing my bare skin, sending shivers to my toes. He repeats with the other shoulder, still holding the towel around us.

Every time he shifts, his lower half moves against mine and ... *damn* ... I need more.

I slide my hands free, one to wrap around his back and the other to slip up to his head, drawing his lips to mine, opening my mouth to his, demanding more.

With a groan and a muttered, "Dry enough," he drops the towel and lifts me off my feet, shifting me to the bedroom. But instead of taking me to the bed, he places me on my feet beside it, taking a long, slow breath while his hands rest on my waist and his gaze drinks me in all the way up from my toes: my thighs, my covered chest, and the bra straps so provocatively loose against my arms.

He answers my unspoken question with a smile that makes me burn. "I might drive fast, but this ... I plan to take it slow."

I shiver as his fingertips trace the curve of my hips, traveling in slow strokes across my ribs and beneath my breasts, pausing to drop kisses across my upper chest, finally drawing back to remove my underwear.

My body comes alive beneath his touch. He spends breathless moments exploring every curve, inhaling my gasps with his kisses. He finally lifts me, naked onto the bed, taking care of contraception before joining me there. Then he starts all over again, kissing me all the way from my lips to my calves.

My whole body burns with a powerful need I've never felt before. I'm not sure if I'm going to survive it. I've already allowed myself to feel more than I ever have. I can't let Cain make me feel like this and leave me wanting. This is the part of sex where I always get left behind. I need it to end so I can find a way to come down without breaking into pieces.

I shiver, my breathing rapid, my back arching into his hands. When he shifts closer to me, I act without thought, hooking my leg around his hips and drawing him to me.

He doesn't let me, swiftly defying me by using his strength to pull me into a sitting position.

He kisses my cheek and that's when I realize a tear has slipped from my eyes.

I gasp, mortified. "I'm not a crier."

He runs his thumb across the tear track that says otherwise. His gaze burns with need, but also with care. "Crying isn't weakness."

My heart is breaking. "Then what is it?"

"It's heart. It's strength." He pulls me closer, shifting me so that I'm straddling his kneeling legs, our bodies still separated but the inside of my thighs pressed against his muscles. "You deserve so much, Archer."

He supports my head and hips as he tips me gently

backward. He whispers against my lips: "I want to make you feel everything good."

A moan escapes my lips when our bodies join and sensation floods me, not elusive, not distant, not a possibility, but real, crashing, overpowering...

I tip my head back against the pillow, wrap my legs around him, and let my body move with his. The need in his eyes is intense. His kisses demand more from me with every stroke inside me, but he controls our movements, focused solely on me. A pure burn flows through me, radiating out from every touch of his lips and hands, the connection between us building until it threatens to tear me apart.

I want everything. I want Cain in my life. I want to be free from my past, free to make my own choices. I want to be Grace and I want to be Archer and I want the power inside me...

This power.

It strikes through me, a deep force. My back shifts, but this time it doesn't hurt. I cry out as need bursts inside me. I arch into Cain, drawing him deeper, thrumming and spiraling as wave after wave draws me upward.

I shatter around him, emotion and sensation exploding. Cain draws me close, as close as we can get, and follows me into the force we've created.

Descending, I open my eyes to meet his, our bodies locked together. I'm shivering; my chest heaves against his. His heartbeat is rapid beneath my palm. He drops kisses onto my cheeks and forehead, but when he draws away from me I catch him and kiss him back, tasting his mouth, inhaling his rapid breaths.

I smile against his mouth, lock my legs around his hips, and whisper, "Again."

A slow smile spreads across his face, lighting his eyes.

He says, "Hmm," but this time it means "Yes."

CHAPTER SEVENTEEN

A long time later, we lie tangled in the sheets, my leg hooked over Cain's hips as I rest plastered against him. He draws my hand up between us and kisses each of my fingertips, one after the other.

His assassin's ring glints. I splay my fingertips, pressing our palms together. His focus shifts to his ring, a small smile curving his lips. "You thought I was married."

I shift against him, allowing my eyes to narrow in a challenge. "It looks like a wedding band."

"Well, then..." He answers me with a challenging look of his own, his eyebrows arched at me, his lips compressed to smother a smile as he slides the ring off his forefinger.

To my shock, he slides it onto his ring finger, saying, "Consider me taken."

I gasp. Swallow. Pain floods me, devouring all the security I felt moments before. It's like an angry wolf come to mangle everything I want. Cain is too perceptive to miss my reaction. His arms quickly slide around me, his big palms flex against my back, soothing strokes calming me.

He says, "I'm not asking for anything, Archer. I'm offering. You have a difficult journey ahead of you. I want you to know that I'll be there for you. I'm on this path with you, heart and soul."

He has already shown me in so many ways that he isn't going to disappear on me, no matter what happens. I'm painfully aware that he is headed toward a battle with Slade Baines that could cost him his life.

I also know that I would choose to die before I let that happen.

If Cain is right, then choosing to die ... could end me.

"How can you...?" I stumble over what I need to ask him. "How can you feel this way about me when I don't even understand what I am."

He contemplates me for a moment, stroking his hand down my side, giving me goosebumps. "If you're Keres, then your mother was too. What do you remember about her?"

"Nothing," I whisper. "I never knew her. Sometimes I wonder if she existed at all." I swallow a humorless laugh. "Actually, Dad once told me this stupid story about how I flew in on the wings of a silver stork. Like I was delivered to him out of the blue. I think it's because he never really wanted me..."

Cain's hands pause on my back. A curious frown forms on his forehead. "What was the story?"

I consider his cautious question, the sudden stillness of his body, the way he is holding his breath.

I'm not sure that I want to tell him. "Dad would say..."

My father's harsh voice echoes back at me ... a cigarette dangling from his fingers, a dagger resting on his knee as if he would flip it around and stab me with it if he had the choice...

"One day, you flew in on the wings of a silver stork. The stork said to me, "Look after this baby and I will make all your ambitions a reality." Of course I fucking agreed. Then the stork turned into a wily fox that devoured all my enemies. In return, all I had to do was keep you alive. Happy was not part of the deal. Just alive."

I come back to myself, the story lingering on my tongue.

Cain is suddenly pale and still. I don't think I've ever seen him look like this. It's such a foreign expression that I'm struggling to identify it as ... *fear*.

He whispers, "The silver stork became a wily fox..."

I don't like the way he is suddenly frozen. "What is it, Cain?"

He swallows. "Your father was Patrick Ryan, the man who ruled Boston's underground under the protection of the assassin known as the Glass Fox."

I say, "Yes. Until she died."

Cain suddenly grips me tightly, his entire body tense. "Damn."

"Cain ... you're scaring me."

"I can't believe I missed it. That explains why... *Damn...*" He closes his eyes, calms, but it's deliberate and forced. As desperate as I am for answers, I give him the moment he needs.

When he opens his eyes, his expression is shuttered. "Lady Tirelli will stop at nothing to get to you. She has been looking for you ever since you were a baby. Ever since she killed your mother."

My world spins. Then anger spirals upward inside me. "She killed my mother? How do you know that?"

He says, "There's truth in your father's story: the Glass Fox saved you when your mother was killed. She hid you with Patrick Ryan. Lady Tirelli has been searching for you ever since. She didn't know you were the baby she wanted, but now ... I think she's figured it out."

He didn't answer my question. In fact, his response is riddled with mysteries, like ... why Lady Tirelli killed my mother. Why she wants me. How Cain knows about any of it. The story I told him only goes so far. There are things he's not telling me, secrets hiding behind his carefully masked expression.

I sink into the bed, my body heavy. My thoughts are still spinning but they keep coming back to one thing ... "Are you telling me that Patrick Ryan wasn't my father?"

A muscle in Cain's jaw flexes. "I'm sorry, Archer. I think he was trying to say as much."

A sob tears out of me. I wrap my arms around myself, curling my knees to my chest, forcing myself away from Cain and into my own protective cocoon. "Good. I hated that bastard and his cigarettes and his daggers ... and his anger. Always forcing me to fight..." I press my hands against my arms.

Cain rears up over me, casting his big body around me, pulling me into his arms. "Nobody makes you do anything you don't want to do. Ever again. Do you hear me?"

I want to believe him. More than anything. But the mysteries about my past are a deadly weight in my heart.

I ask, "If the Keres are supposed to be invincible, how did Lady Tirelli kill my mother?"

Cain's arms tighten around me. "Assassin's magic. You have to stay away from anyone wearing an assassin's ring."

I shudder. That includes Lutz Logan and Slade

Baines. I meet Cain's eyes, my focus flicking to his ring. "What about you?"

He kisses me, demanding my focus, stroking my arms and back, his hands finding all the spots that make me forget everything.

"Except me."

CHAPTER EIGHTEEN

I fix the glittering necklace in place around my neck, mentally preparing myself for the ceremony that starts in half an hour. I got up this morning, put my contact lenses in, and ate my breakfast while reading a book, just like normal. Then I went out and trained Juliet, also like normal. When I came back to Cain's quarters to eat lunch, I discovered that eating was the furthest thing from his mind, so my afternoon was ... wonderfully *not* routine.

Now my hands shake. Somehow I managed to get through the day without remembering that everything I believed about myself has been tipped on its head. I am not Patrick Ryan's daughter. I am not entirely human. Lady Tirelli killed my mother and she's after me, not only because of my reputation, but for some mysterious reason that Cain can't explain.

But worse than that ... Slade Baines will arrive tomorrow and Cain will fight him. Fear is a quiet whisper in the back of my mind. Doubt is a sharp claw in my stomach.

Lutz Logan is coming to the ceremony tonight, along with the woman Cain calls "the Guardian." All I have to do is walk out of the Realm with Lutz tonight and I can be certain that Cain is safe.

That's if these heels don't break my ankles.

I growl at the impossible shoes, catch a flicker of movement in the mirror, and spin to find Cain lounging in the doorway. It's the first time in days that he has crept up on me. His gaze devours me with a hunger I wasn't expecting.

I thought he would be dressed in a suit, but far from it. His hair is slicked back and armor hugs his body, sleek copper plates custom-made to conform to his broad shoulders and chest. The color contrasts with his eyes, making them even more piercing. It also matches the gold in his assassin's ring. Each armored plate is interwoven to allow full movement, which he demonstrates when he plucks me off my feet with a husky whisper: "How soon can you take this dress off?"

I laugh. "Quicker than you can get out of that."

The armor is cold and I shiver against it. He quickly puts me down. "Not soon enough."

We take the stairs to the first floor. Cain told me

that the ceremony will be held in the main hall of the Cathedral and that the Novices are allowed in for the first and only time before they become Superiors.

Juliet greets us halfway along the corridor, dressed in an evening gown that hugs her petite form, her light brown hair piled atop her head.

She murmurs to me, "The woman you're about to meet is the Guardian. She has a name, but we're not allowed to use it. A representative from each of the Factions is also here: Lutz Logan from the Legion, and the Dominion Master, Alexei Mason."

"Is it unusual for another Master to be here?"

"No. Actually, it's more unusual that Slade Baines isn't here."

Cain twitches beside me. He and I both know it's because Cain asked Slade for time. The minute Slade steps foot in the Horde's Realm, the two Masters will be required to settle the score. Juliet doesn't know about it. Not yet.

Juliet leads us to an anteroom located before the main entrance. As I pass through the door, goosebumps rise on my skin. It's like walking through a spray of water.

Juliet murmurs, "This room is a sub-Realm. Nobody outside can hear or see us."

Inside, a woman and two men wait for us. Although they are all dressed in evening attire, a quick check tells me that they are all wearing assassin's rings. Juliet bows to them, but doesn't lower her eyes. I remember Cain telling me that this is how the Factions greet each other.

Cain takes up position behind and to my right, the same protective location he used with Parker the day I first saw them in the café.

The woman steps forward and there's no doubt in my mind that she is the Guardian. Her caramel hair falls straight to her waist, a forest-green evening gown accentuating her brown eyes. Her ring is a silver band adorned with diamonds and a cluster of emeralds in the shape of leaves. She is regal and serene in a way that I could never be.

She says, "Hello, dear. You must be Archer. I want to thank you for saving Briar's life. Because of you, we did not have to mourn a friend. I'm genuinely sorry it will come at great cost for you."

Cain stiffens beside me, but the Guardian ignores his reaction, inclining her head at him. "Good evening, Cain. Are you well?"

"I am. Thank you, Guardian."

Lutz hangs back, his amber eyes never leaving me, as if he's determined to keep me in his sights now that I'm here. But the enormous man beside him has no such hesitation, addressing me directly. "Archer Ryan, you're lucky to be alive."

He is a full head taller than Cain, making me tilt my head back to see him. I'm not used to it. With a shaved head, stormy gray eyes, and a nose that looks like it has been hit too many times, this man oozes threat. A jet-black ring set with chunky rubies glimmers on his hand.

I thought Lutz was threatening, but Alexei Mason is a man I would not want to cross. I quickly judge his weight and balance, settling into my own casually defensive stance.

"Luck had nothing to do with it, Dominion Master," I say. "If you'd like, I can give you a demonstration."

He breaks into a grin, looking down at me through the slits of his cold-as-ice eyes. "I like her, Cain. Make sure Slade doesn't kill her."

He turns a surprising glare on Cain, who replies, "Anyone who comes after Archer answers to me."

Cain's pinpoint focus is Lutz. The amber-eyed assassin folds his arms across his chest, a sharp growl sounding in his chest. "I will do my duty under the Code no matter how hated I am. The Code protects us all."

Cain clenches his teeth and takes a step forward, but the Guardian quickly intervenes.

"Well," she says with a breezy smile. "Now that we're all suitably tense, let's get on with the evening, shall we?"

She takes Cain's arm as she glides past, firmly sweeping him along with her.

Cain catches my hand and gives it a squeeze before letting it go. Juliet falls in beside me, but she's frowning.

I murmur, "What is it?"

"Your name."

"Oh." With a start, I remember that Juliet knows me as Grace, but they all called me "Archer." "I'm sorry I couldn't tell you."

She casts a worried glance back at Lutz and Alexei. "It explains a few things. But it also means you're in danger."

I give her a wry smile. "Just a little."

She stops speaking as we enter the corridor and head toward the meeting hall. Men and women dressed in suits and evening gowns mingle around dinner tables. I recognize the Novices, as well as Brenna, who wears a glittering silver gown. At least twenty other men and women stand around tables, but I take note that nobody else is wearing an assassin's ring. That means the only true dangers are the Guardian, Lutz, and Alexei, and I know they will all abide by the Code.

I force myself to relax.

The room is decorated with golden chandeliers, majestic tapestries hanging from the walls depicting male and female champions. The gathering looks for all the world like a social ball, not a meeting of killers preparing to welcome their new Master.

Everyone quiets as we enter. With a small smile, Juliet breaks off from me. "I'll see you later."

Brenna approaches our group, casting glares at Juliet, who holds her head high and ignores her. I squash my instinctive dislike when Brenna falls in beside Lutz and Alexei, seeming content to glare daggers at me. As Cain's second-in-command, she will sit with us tonight.

I'm painfully aware of all the stares as I follow Cain to a table at the front where an imposing man waits for us. He is older, tall, and slightly gray at the temples.

Everyone else seems to know him. Lutz and Alexei bow while Cain gives him a respectful nod.

The man addresses me: "I am Abraham Kolko, former Master of the Horde. Well met, Archer Ryan."

Well, I guess that cat is out of the bag.

His statement startles everyone within earshot. The nearby assassins look me up and down, some with curiosity, some with open aggression. I guess I'm lucky my name was never written in their ledgers. It's probably just a matter of time.

A sharp inhale behind me is followed by a deep growl. My quick glance tells me that Brenna backed away from me when she heard my name, but she stepped into Alexei Mason in the process. She turns bright red as he picks her up off his toes and places her away from him. I nearly feel sorry for her.

I return my attention to the former Horde Master. "It's a pleasure, Abraham."

I hold out my hand, an action that draws shocked gasps from everyone around me. *Oops.* I guess assassins don't make physical contact.

I take a deep breath. "Since I'm not an assassin, I thought we might greet each other with common courtesy. After all, we are simply two killers meeting for the first time. We have no quarrel with each other … do we?"

He takes my hand, his grip firm. "No, we do not."

We let go of each other and the room exhales.

The Guardian takes Cain's arm again. "Come with me please, Cain Carter."

Cain waits while I take a seat before he follows the Guardian onto the dais. I end up seated with Alexei on one side of me and Abraham on the other. Brenna sits on the opposite side, choosing to locate herself beside Lutz, side-eyeing him as if she thinks he could be an ally. Whatever she says to him, he answers with narrowed eyes and a sharp rebuttal. It obviously takes more than a title and a sideways comment to earn his respect.

Alexei's deep voice is like rumbling thunder beside me. "I'm curious, Archer Ryan, how it turns out that you're a woman."

I can't help but smile. "Would you believe you're the first assassin to ask me that, Dominion Master?"

He says, "Call me 'Alexei.' I prefer my name when I'm among friends."

Friends, huh? I'm not sure what I've done to deserve that label other than brazenly challenging him before.

I raise my eyebrows. "Well, then, you can call me 'Grace.'"

He continues to grin at me. "You didn't answer my question."

"That's correct."

He blinks at me, his jaw dropping a little. "Well, now I really like you. Cain had better keep you alive."

My smile fades. For some reason, Alexei's frankness appeals to me. Beneath his ferocious exterior, I sense deep intelligence. I check Brenna before I speak, noting that she has turned her chair away and is now in deep conversation with an assassin sitting at the table behind her.

I dare to speak my thoughts when I say to Alexei, "Cain thinks he can win against Slade."

"But you aren't so sure."

"I've never met Slade Baines. Could *you* beat him?"

Alexei laughs. "Hell, no. I tried that once. It didn't go well." His laughter fades. "The hardest part about being an assassin is watching people you care about get hurt and not being able to do a damn thing about it."

I don't know what event he might be talking about, but I recognize honesty when I hear it. "Then I should do whatever I can to make sure a battle between Cain and Slade doesn't happen."

Alexei contemplates me for a moment. "As unhappy as it makes me ... that would be wise."

I study my hands as the Guardian calls everyone to attention and a hush falls over the gathering. When I raise my eyes to the dais, I find Cain watching me from where he stands beside her. It surprises me that I spoke so openly to Alexei about my feelings. I've always kept my thoughts to myself, but I can't regret what I said. I won't hide the fact that I care about Cain or that I will do anything to keep him alive.

I just can't allow myself to recognize that ... perhaps ... Cain would do the same for me.

Cain suddenly pauses on stage, placing his hand on the Guardian's arm, indicating the far end of the room. I swivel in the direction that has taken his focus to see two women standing in the doorway. One is Sarah and the other...

Parker strides confidently toward the front of the room, her head held high, her flowing A-line dress swishing against her long legs. Unlike me, she knows how to walk in heels.

Lutz stands up as soon as she approaches our table, stepping back and quietly indicating his seat. Abraham and Alexei also politely stand.

Parker tips her head to acknowledge Lutz's

gesture, murmuring, "Thank you, Lutz Logan," before she glides into the seat he vacated.

Lutz promptly strides across the room and positions himself against the side wall, a quiet sentry now.

Parker folds her hands in her lap, ignores Brenna scowling beside her, and raises her eyes to the stage.

She gives Cain a small smile.

Cain can't hide his emotions, a smile breaking across his face.

He throws his shoulders back, a weight lifting visibly as the Guardian holds her hand out, palm up. Cain places his in hers.

She misses a beat at the position of his assassin's ring, casts him a quick curious glance, but says, "Cain Carter, will you uphold the Assassin's Code, follow the Code, and die by the Code?"

Cain inhales. "I will."

"Then I sanction your appointment as Horde Master."

"Thank you, Guardian."

The gathering breaks into applause and many of the assassins rise to their feet. Whatever distrust exists between Cain and Brenna, it doesn't seem to be reflected in his reception by his Faction.

Alexei murmurs beside me, "Cain's fate is now sealed."

I ask, "That's it? That's the ceremony?"

He grins. "Assassins get right to the point."

The cheering finally dies down while Cain and the Guardian descend from the dais. Brenna shows her first sign of humanity when she swaps seats so that Cain can sit beside Parker, although I suspect she was dying to get away from her anyway.

Cain is very circumspect around Parker, giving her space and allowing her to direct their conversation. Halfway through the meal, she reaches for his hand and bumps her shoulder against his, leaning in. I don't have the power to hear what she murmurs to him, and I wish they had privacy to say what they need to say, but Cain responds by squeezing her hand.

Parker shines a smile at him and for a moment … everything is okay.

Then two things happen at once: Lutz Logan lifts himself off the far wall, a sudden frown descending over his face, and Brenna excuses herself from our table.

A moment later, Lutz shoots into action, breaking into a run.

He roars, "Get down!"

I flinch as bullets spray our table.

CHAPTER NINETEEN

*P*ain explodes across my shoulder. Blood splatters the tabletop and Abraham hits it face-first, his dead eyes turned in my direction.

Too far away to reach me, Cain shouts, "Archer, get down!"

At the same time, he dives in front of Parker, grabs the Guardian, and pulls them both to the floor.

A scream wrenches out of me, but it's a reflex, an exhalation of fear, leaving me cold inside. I shove Abraham off the table and grab the edge of it.

Alexei's big hands close over mine, helping me tip the furniture and swing it around as a shield. He propels me behind it a moment before bullets tear into the spot where we were standing.

From one side of the room to the other, the remaining assassins tip furniture to form shields.

Wood splinters and bullets thunder against our table, threatening to tear it apart.

Lutz slides in behind us and Cain curls around Parker. Cain uses his body as a shield around her while she keeps her head down, huddling beside him.

His ferocious eyes meet mine, swiftly assessing me for damage. I dive against Alexei, angling my shoulder away from Cain. The minute he sees I'm hurt, he'll come after me, but he has to protect Parker.

My wound is a distraction he doesn't need.

Cain roars at Lutz, louder than the gunfire. "Who did you see?"

Lutz snarls, "Your own people. The Novices."

The Guardian startles from her position on the other side of Cain. She winces as a bullet bites off a chunk of wood on her side. "A coup?"

Cain grits his teeth, pale with rage. *"Brenna."*

The Guardian reaches into her bodice and pulls out a hair tie, ignoring the thundering gunfire around us. My eyes widen as she shimmies out of her dress to reveal a protective suit beneath it. She untucks multiple flaps, pulls them up to cover her chest and neck, and zips it up. It now covers her from her neck to her ankles.

Beside me, Alexei also pulls off his tie and suit to reveal his own assassin's suit. He throws his shirt upward where the bullets shred it. His grin is cold, making me shudder. "Just for fun."

When I turn around, Lutz has already rid himself of his formal clothing, zipping up his own protective suit. He scoots closer to Cain, reaching for Parker. "Let me take Parker to safety."

Cain's response is instinctive. "Stay away from her or so help me—"

Lutz's fist whips out, thumping Cain full in the face. "Listen to me! I can get her to safety. You can't!"

Cain barely reacts to the punch, growling back at Lutz, but the Guardian shouts, "Cain! Lutz won't let anything happen to Parker. You have my word on it."

Meanwhile Parker pushes at her brother. "It's okay, Cain."

He stares at her in shock as she struggles to make him release her.

She says, "I'm a liability if I stay. I need to go, and I trust Lutz."

"You … what?"

She opens her mouth. Shuts it again. "I'm going with him. Give them hell, brother."

She scrambles out of Cain's arms and barrels into Lutz, who wraps his arms around her and turns so that his back is in the line of fire. He crouches low with her, protecting her head with his big arms.

A second later, they disappear. Blurred.

To fit behind the table, I'm pressed up against Alexei, suddenly conscious of his big chest against my side. He's shielding me because I don't have a protective suit. He's also concealing my wound and ... I think he knows it.

I raise my eyes to his, silently begging him not to say anything. There are other assassins who aren't wearing suits who need Cain's help. I can't be a distraction. I sure as hell don't want Brenna to win this fight and ... it's time to test Cain's theory about what I am. If he's right, then bullets can't kill me. The wound certainly doesn't hurt as much as I expected.

Alexei murmurs in my ear, "No suit, huh?"

"Just a dress." I take hold of the hem and rip it up to my thigh to maximize leg movement. Then I slip off my heels, all while staying curled up beside him. "But I could stab someone's eyes out with these." I laugh, a kind of cold panic filling my veins. "Don't worry about me, Alexei. I've survived a lot worse."

He tips his head. "I might worry a little."

Talking to Alexei keeps me from acknowledging Cain's drawn features, the way he's focused on me, and the fact that I'm completely unprotected with no guarantees that I'm anything more than human.

The Guardian has pulled her hair back now, her assassin's ring glowing, casting emerald light around her body.

She is cold as stone as she says, "Each Novice is complicit in the death of Abraham Kolko, former Horde Master. They have broken the first rule of the

Assassin's Code, for which the penalty is death. Who will kill them?"

"I will," Cain growls.

"And I will assist," Alexei promises.

The Guardian nods. "Sanctioned."

Alexei grins like a wolf about to eat dinner. He raises his voice to Cain. "Archer is prepared to fight. How about you, brother?"

Cain takes a deep breath, a dangerous calm settling around him, but his gaze remains on me. "I'm ready."

With a roar, he stands up into the gunfire, golden light flowing around his body, the bullets streaming off him like leaves in a waterfall. My eyes widen as he takes off at a run, the Guardian hot on his heels. She stays within the slipstream of the shield he created.

Alexei places a firm hand on my arm to stop me before I can follow them. "There is no shame in staying where you are safe, Archer."

I laugh. "If I'm dead, Cain's problems go away."

"Something tells me he doesn't see you as a problem." He examines my shoulder now that Cain isn't watching. "It's a clean exit wound. You have maybe half an hour before you collapse from blood loss. Less if you're running around."

"Then I'd better use my time wisely."

"Here." Alexei reaches for his discarded shirt and wraps it tightly around my shoulder. He is matter-of-fact. "This will give you longer. Seek shelter when your vision starts to blur. You won't have long after that. But hopefully we can get you help before then."

I shake my head. "You're tending the wound of a dead woman. I either die tonight or I die tomorrow."

He nods. "It's time to choose."

I say, "I choose the path that keeps Cain alive."

I close my eyes so I don't have to see Alexei's pity. I focus instead on listening for the bullets, sensing the direction from which they're coming—near the entrance. Brenna must be blocking the escape there. Lutz is sure to have taken Parker out the back. Other assassins are also fleeing in that direction, running from table to table. I catch sight of Sarah among them, running to safety. What I know of their code tells me that only Cain and Alexei are sanctioned to kill the Novices, so there's no point in the others staying to die.

We are the only ones running into the battle.

A sudden gap in the spray tells me that Cain and the Guardian must have reached the attackers.

I dart out from behind the table and Alexei follows close behind me. Unlike Cain, he doesn't create a shield around himself and I wonder briefly if he can't. I don't know enough about assassin's magic to know if everyone's is the same.

In the distance, Cain plows into a group of five Novices. He grabs the first weapon he can reach, twists it, disarms the Novice, and slams him with a fist so hard that the man's face caves in. I suck in a sharp breath while my feet pound the floor. If that's the sort of damage Cain can do, it makes me realize how strong the Jaguars were. And yet I wrestled one to the ground and broke its jaw.

Another Novice screams when Cain's boot meets his ribs, and a third doesn't have time to draw breath before Cain snaps his neck.

Now that Cain is fighting hand to hand, his shield is down and his back is vulnerable. The other Novices scatter and locate themselves behind two tables, one on either side of the fight, attempting to get a clear shot at Cain.

Not if I can help it.

I draw the attention of one group with a shout, zigzagging toward them while Alexei attacks the other. He flings his hand out, ebony darts forming in the air and spearing toward the attackers, taking down half of them in one sweep. The others try to take cover, but Alexei crashes into them, his own version of hand-to-hand combat even more brutal than Cain's.

On my side, multiple gun barrels follow my movements as I run toward the Novices, projectiles sweeping the air beside me, but I avoid them until ... a bullet hits me. Straight in the heart.

Pain explodes through my chest as the bullet enters and swiftly exits my body. I miss a step, anticipate death, expect to fall but...

I sense the continuing *thud-thud* of my most precious internal organ.

Well, what do you know?

I should be dead but I'm not.

My heart keeps beating and I keep running. Alexei gives me a brief glance from a distance, cursory enough to make me think he believes the shot missed me.

Another bullet flies past me, this one from behind me, taking down two of the Novices who were firing at me. From the corner of my eye, I catch sight of Juliet kneeling behind a table to my far left, her weapon carefully aimed.

I leap the table and plow into the Novice who fired the shot into my heart. I recognize this guy as the one who bullied Juliet. He pulls the trigger as I crash into him—a shot through my ribs that doesn't stop me.

The others shout, confused that I'm still moving, but I am faster than ever, a whirlwind of movement, as if being closer to death gives me fuel, energy I didn't have before. I grab the guy's gun with one hand, thump him with the other, flip the weapon, and follow his fall to the ground with a bullet to the head. Then I whirl, disarm two more and end them both.

"Novices! Haul back!" Brenna's sudden shout causes the Novices to rush toward her. Only four of them remain.

Alexei takes up position beside Cain, two giants

waiting to annihilate their enemies. The Guardian stands beside them, and Juliet strides forward to join them. As soon as Cain looks for me, I rush to position myself beside Alexei, a step back and to his left, making sure I'm out of Cain's line of sight—Alexei's too. The blood pooling on my chest is a dead giveaway that I've been shot.

Brenna continues to shout as she approaches from the doorway: "Horde Master, you are hereby challenged."

Cain's big chest rises and falls, his features filled with battle rage. "You're no match for me, Brenna."

She laughs. "Oh, I'm not going to fight you."

A figure walks behind her, lithe and graceful, emerging from the shadows like a predator slinking out of the dark. The newcomer is entirely covered in a protective suit. Only her eyes are visible.

Cain's rage instantly becomes more intense, pinpoint.

I frown at the newcomer, my eyes suddenly watering. With her arrival, the scent of roses wafts up my nose and sticks, heavy and repugnant. Roses are meant to be beautiful, but what I sense beneath the scent is foul, like something rotting.

Brenna smiles at Cain. "I believe you know Lady Tirelli."

I suck in a sharp breath. Rage and fear storm inside me. My instincts scream at me to step forward and fight her. I may have hated Patrick Ryan, but he was the only father I knew and she killed him.

Cain's voice is hard as granite as he addresses Brenna. "You brought Lady Tirelli into the Realm."

Brenna shrugs. "If you die, I win the Horde."

The Guardian speaks up, her scathing response like ice: "Any assassin can challenge a Master. Nobody has ever been stupid enough to try."

Brenna snarls, "Lady Tirelli is my proxy—"

The Lady herself interrupts, speaking in a voice that reminds me of a waterfall, soft and lulling. Almost … beautiful. It sings into my ears, tugging at me as her focus lands on me. "Archer Ryan, you will come with me."

Cain steps between us, blocking my view. I'm grateful he doesn't look back. I may be standing upright, but the front of my dress isn't in good shape. It seems I can survive bullets, but my body is taking its sweet time healing the wounds.

"Stand aside, Cain." Lady Tirelli glides closer to him. "And I won't hunt down your sister."

Brenna interjects, "Wait … you won't fight him? That's not our deal!"

Lady Tirelli's hand snakes out. She grabs Brenna by the throat, pulling her close and squeezing her neck. "You've outlived your usefulness."

Brenna gasps. Flails. Her eyes pop wide. She gasps for air, her face turning red as she chokes.

Her neck snaps.

Lady Tirelli throws Brenna to the side. Her lifeless body flops to the floor. The remaining Novices scream and shout, start running, but Lady Tirelli twists in their direction, pinning them with a glare. They jolt to a stop, falling silent, and crowd against the wall, all of them eyeing the door. They're dead if they don't get out of here. If Lady Tirelli doesn't kill them, Cain will. I find it hard to pity them. Brenna led them astray, but they demonstrated their cruel natures when they tried to hurt Parker on the first day.

Lady Tirelli says, "Move, Cain. Or watch your world burn."

"No."

He takes a battle stance, pulling out one of his daggers, preparing to fight her.

Her eyes narrow. "Many have fought me. None have succeeded."

I squeeze my eyes closed. I've spent my life hiding. I hid behind my name for sixteen years, becoming a faceless myth. For the last four years I've hidden behind aliases, never staying anywhere long. This week was the first time I didn't hide. I was happy … the best week of my life.

Reality is only a step away.

I draw my shoulders back, deliberately undoing the shirt from my arm. Blood flows down it and I let it drip as I take each step I need to take. Cain said that the Keres can choose to die. If I am one of them, I will choose to bleed out before I do anything this woman wants.

I step out from behind Cain.

Lady Tirelli's smile becomes so wide that it's visible beneath her gauzy face mask.

Cain grabs me, inhaling, eyes wide, but his concern is not my destination. "You're hurt!"

I whisper, "Whatever she wants, she won't have me for long."

"No—"

I place my hand over his heart. "This woman ended my father, despite protection from the Glass Fox, despite an army of men. She can get to anyone. I won't let her hurt Parker."

He believes me. There is not a shred of doubt in his eyes, as if he has already seen firsthand the damage Lady Tirelli can do. But the set of his lips, the way his expression begs me not to take another step...

He would have fought for me.

I meet his eyes. "Thank you. For everything. For making my life ... mean something for a little while."

I turn away from him, my hand slipping from his chest, but he catches it, holding tight another moment.

Lady Tirelli's greeting is like honey. "I've waited twenty years to meet you, little sparrow. The Glass Fox was clever to hide you with Patrick Ryan." She scoffs. "He was the most unlikely father."

She greets me like a mother would greet her daughter, taking my shoulders in her hands, gazing at me with lustrous hazel eyes. She doesn't seem to notice that her thumb slides through the blood covering my shoulder.

She tucks my hair behind my ears, cooing at me, "Beautiful girl, come with me."

Her grip is firm around my free hand. She is made of steel beneath her soft exterior. Holding onto me, she turns, expecting me to follow her, but Cain is still holding my other hand, and his fingers tighten, tugging me to a stop.

For the very first time … he doesn't let me go.

Surprise shoots through me as I twist back. He has always allowed me to make my own choices. "Cain?"

He shakes his head, a slow, dangerous side to side motion, his lips pressed together in determination, his piercing eyes filled with fire. "I won't let you die, Archer."

CHAPTER TWENTY

ain's focus shifts to Lady Tirelli. Rage floods his face, a glow building around him a second before he drops my hand and charges at her.

She whirls, gasps, and quickly digs her heels in, letting me go so she can get her fists up.

Cain drops his shoulder. Instead of hitting her, he picks her off her feet, his big arms clamping around her thighs, flipping and throwing her. She has nowhere to go but down, landing on her shoulder with a crunch. She rolls through it, recovering quickly, jumping back to her feet several paces away.

Cain flips a dagger into each hand, slashing at her face as she ducks and steps rapidly to avoid the cuts. She rallies and fights back, her fists crashing into him, knocking the daggers wide without touching them.

One of them narrowly misses my face, but I know better than to touch it.

Oomph. Alexei is a blur as he barrels into me, picks me up, and carries me out of harm's way. His commanding voice orders me, "Stay out of this fight."

Cain hits back, but so does Lady Tirelli. Their fists fly, magic streaming around them, the impact between them like iron gavels. Each time he connects with the fist on which he wears his assassin's ring, she winces, reacting defensively.

I struggle against Alexei's hold, my eyes narrowing as I realize that Cain's fists don't cause Lady Tirelli pain, but his magic does. This is more than a fist-fight. Even so, she is incredibly strong.

"I have to help!"

Alexei growls in my ear, "You have to stay."

As soon as the fight started, the remaining four Novices took off, disappearing through the door, but they are the least of my worries.

On the other side of the room, the Guardian and Juliet steer clear of the fight. The Guardian jolts every time Cain hits Lady Tirelli. I remember what Cain told me about assassinations: they must be sanctioned.

I stare at her, willing her to shout out that she sanctions Lady Tirelli's death—can't she do that?—but she remains silent.

I stop struggling against Alexei and demand, "Why

doesn't the Guardian sanction the kill? She sanctioned the deaths of the Novices."

Alexei says, "The Novices are assassins who broke the first rule. When an assassin breaks the Code, the Guardian can step in. But Lady Tirelli is not an assassin. Her death can only be sanctioned if her name is written in Cain's ledger."

"There's no time to do that..." I twist, struggling harder. "What happens if Cain kills her without sanction?"

"He will be excommunicated. That means he is no longer protected from other assassins. We are a vicious people. Those who leave do not last long. Cain will be dead within a week."

A cry builds in my chest. "I have to stop him. I can't let him do this."

A crack makes my stomach turn. Cain's wrist dangles. It's the hand on which he wears the ring. Lady Tirelli smiles when he drops his arm to protect his wounded limb. It gives her the opening she must have been waiting for. Her next hit is hard enough to twist his body sideways, crashing him to the floor.

"Let me go!" I draw on all my strength to push out of Alexei's arms, then catch his look of surprise that I succeed, before I race across the distance.

Lady Tirelli picks Cain up by his collar, pulling his torso off the floor. The way his head rocks back tells me he is unconscious.

She raises her fist, preparing to end him, and there is not a damn thing any of the assassins in the room can do to stop her. The Guardian screams and Juliet's hand flies over her mouth.

I crash into Lady Tirelli, both arms outstretched, pushing her backward. She lets go of Cain and tumbles across the floor, trying to get back to her feet. I hook my leg under Cain's shoulders before his head hits the ground, sliding my knees under him as fast as I can. His beautiful head settles into my lap. *Thank God, he's breathing.*

I place him gently onto the floor and rise to stand between him and Lady Tirelli, my arms splayed. My voice is guttural. "Touch Cain again and I will crush you. The assassins aren't allowed to kill you, but I am."

I sense Alexei hurry up behind me to pull Cain clear, dragging him across the floor to the Guardian. As soon as Alexei looks like he's going to run back to help me, she grabs him with a firm shake of her head. "No."

Alexei curses. Twists back to me. Curses again. But he stays put.

None of the assassins can act against Lady Tirelli, no matter what she does. *Damn their rules.*

But rules never applied to me. I assess my surroundings, the weapons that might be available to me, while I draw on the memory of every dirty fight I ever fought, every dirty trick I used against an opponent. Steak knives, forks, shattered pieces of table wood. I'm not afraid of splinters in my fingers.

Lady Tirelli recovers, drawing herself upright. "You can try, little sparrow."

I let her confidence wash over me. The first chance I get, I'm ripping that face mask off her. I feint left, duck under her fist, and land a solid hit to her stomach, followed by a quick kick to the back of her legs. She cries out, the first sign of pain all evening, as her legs give way. She rights herself before she loses her balance, but the way she stumbles tells me her legs are her weak point. *Good. I'll use them against her.*

I snatch up the steak knife I was aiming for and hurl it straight toward her neck. She dodges it at the last minute and it slices past her shoulder instead.

She strides toward me, swinging quick blows, but I glide around her, avoiding her fists, fluid like Cain taught me. Another quick kick against her legs sends her crashing into the nearest table.

Cain told me that the Keres were the perfect killers —and the perfect protectors. I snatch up a dropped fork, run toward Lady Tirelli, leap off the table she bumped into, and slam the fork into the shoulder I nicked. She screams, this time with rage. The angrier she gets, the more mistakes she will make. I spin out of her reach, but not before I snatch up the tablecloth, rapidly twisting it in my hands as she rages after me, the fork still protruding from her body.

She's smart. This way she won't bleed out.

I allow her to connect once to my stomach, because she will expect me to bend, which I do, but only because it's the perfect position to break her kneecaps with my fists.

She screams and drops, flailing as I land on her stomach. When she lashes out, I catch her wrist and wrap the cloth around it, catching her next punch and tying that hand tight too, jumping to my feet and yanking her arms above her head. My foot meets her face. Shame I'm not wearing heels.

She spits blood and pulls against the makeshift rope, rolling and wrapping herself in it. I let it go, picking up a piece of wood instead, following her as she jumps to her feet. I don't give her time to recover before I ram it into her stomach.

Wobbling on her feet, she tries to pull it out. "You fight like a demon!"

I kick her stomach, hands and all, to drive the stake deeper.

Shock floods her face. I follow her expression with my fist, smashing it off her face.

Her blood sprays across me.

She stumbles backward, her chest heaving, trying to disentangle herself from the cloth and remove the shard at the same time. "Your kind were never this strong."

Twice now she has implied that she knows what I

am. But if she means she fought a Keres … that means there could be others. There must be others.

Please let me not be alone.

I grind my teeth. "They didn't grow up with Patrick Ryan."

The cloth drops free from her wrists, but she doesn't let it go, whipping it in her fists. I avoid it as I head in for the kill.

As my body goes through the motions, a dull scream grows at the back of my mind. How many more times will I have to be a monster? How many more people will I have to kill with my bare hands in order to survive?

I just need one good hold of her head and I will snap her neck as easily as she snapped Brenna's. I dodge her attempt to capture me with the cloth, punch her stomach, follow her body as she bends, latch onto the side of her head, raise my other hand, ready to twist…

She hisses, "Why haven't you opened your wings?"

I falter. It's only for a second. But it's enough.

She shoves my left hand away from her head, wraps the cloth around it, and whips the rope around my neck. She twists at the same time, kicking the side of my knee, forcing me to the side so she can leverage herself into position behind me.

She kicks the back of my other knee to force me

down, the drop pulling the cloth tighter around my neck, so hard that my vision blurs.

Sudden pain rakes across my shoulders. A sharp object digs into me. The fork? Is she seriously digging for my wings?

Lady Tirelli's voice is urgent, demanding. "Open your wings and you will be able to kill me. That's what you want, isn't it?"

More than anything. I struggle against the rope and her efforts to find my wings, fighting her iron grip on me.

I opt for the truth, wanting to test her reaction. Also to distract her while I position myself to break free. "I can't."

She freezes. "What?"

"I can't open them. They're locked."

"*Can't?*" She shoves away from me so suddenly that I take a tumble.

She charges at me as she screams, "Then you're useless to me!"

I hurry to find my feet and defend myself as she hits out, her arms swinging while I duck each impact, unraveling myself from the cloth at the same time.

When her next hit swings wide, she pulls up short to scream at me, planting her feet. "Twenty years wasted! You're useless! Worthless!"

A week ago, her words would have hit me harder

than any fist. But the last few days with Cain have given me a different perspective about myself.

I say, "I am not worthless."

While she paces, a silver glow builds around her body like the glow I saw around Cain. She must be wearing an assassin's ring that makes her stronger—or helps her heal. That's the only explanation for why she's still standing despite her wounds. That could also explain why Cain's magic had an impact on her—the two magics were colliding. If she has access to assassin's magic, it would certainly explain why her reputation is so formidable.

She snarls, "Well ... if I can't get what I want, then neither can you."

She suddenly stops and throws her hand out, palm up, tugging at the air.

I stare at her, confused, until I follow the direction of her hand.

She's pointing at Cain.

In the distance, a single flame rises up from his body, a glowing orb, brighter than the brightest diamond. It is just like the shifters', but pure and strong. *His soul.*

Lady Tirelli's fingers flex and Cain's soul-flame floats toward her.

A scream builds in my chest. "How did you do that?"

She smiles, her voice a low murmur. "I have ways. I

will crush his soul and you can't stop me unless you release your wings."

"No!" I leap forward, not at her, but to intercept the flame, catching the orb in my hand, holding tight. It beats against my fingers, pulling toward her, but I refuse to let it go.

Lady Tirelli gasps, frowns, her fingers trembling, concentration falling over her features, trying harder to pull Cain's soul toward her, but I don't budge.

To my surprise, she gives up quickly, dropping her arm with a laugh. She leans into me, quietly hissing. "Very well. You win. But what's really going to kill you is that you can't save him unless you release your wings."

She slinks toward the door, turning only to whisper, "He will die now."

Across the room, the Guardian rises from her position beside Cain to stop Alexei before he chases after Lady Tirelli. "Let her go!"

Juliet sags with relief as our enemy disappears into the shadows. The disgusting scent of roses recedes and her absence lifts a weight from me. But panic replaces it. The others don't realize that Cain is dying.

Cain's soul is like a careful tapestry, deep darkness interwoven with bright strands of compassion. He is capable of incredible violence and astonishing kindness. He pulled me out of darkness and showed me another way—he gave me a glimpse of a life with someone who ... loves me.

The flame inside my fist is growing cold.

A sob rises to my throat. My feet move before I know it.

The Guardian approaches me. "Archer? Are you okay?"

I'm certain they didn't hear my conversation with Lady Tirelli about wings, but right now that's the least of my concerns.

"Don't touch me!" My voice breaks. "Cain is dying."

"How do you know—?" She spins back to Cain, dropping to his side to check his pulse, her eyes shooting wide.

Her hand flies over her mouth, smothering a cry. "He's already gone."

Juliet drops to her knees. Alexei freezes. But Cain isn't gone. Not yet.

I rage at them. "Get his armor off. Then get away from him."

When they stare at me in shock, I shout, "I can save him! Do it!"

If I can hold on to his soul then ... *dammit* ... I can give it back.

Alexei hurries to lever Cain onto his side while the Guardian undoes the armor, assisting each other to pull it over his head.

I shout, "Shirt, too!"

I don't have time to go carefully. The first two steps are easy, the next not so much. By the time I kneel beside him, they've ripped off his shirt and hurriedly stepped back, but now I'm pushing against a force that bashes against me, stealing the breath from my lungs. A fire burns in my back, a power that threatens to tear me apart from the inside.

My wings. I sense them writhing, trying to form, like pieces of glass cutting me on the inside.

They can't ... I can't...

I hunch my shoulders, place my free hand over the hand in which I hold Cain's soul, and push with all my might, one slow inch at a time, one painful increment at a time toward his bare chest. The harder I push, the worse the pain grows.

I scream, jolting when agony spears through my stomach, shooting up into my chest, into my heart. It thuds. Slower. As if my life is being consumed by the force inside me with every second that I try to do the impossible.

For the first time in my life, I am not cold.

Heat rises from my arms and the backs of my hands, sweat drips from my forehead and pools at the base of my neck, watery rivers of blood drip from my shoulder and chest where the bullet hit me.

Tears wash down my cheeks. I can't do it ... I'm still too far away...

Cain's soul sputters inside my fist, nearly cold and

gone, and terror fills me. My heartbeats are dying but I have to keep going. My shaking hands nearly touch Cain's chest. His soul is so close to his body.

Nearly ... almost...

As I force my hands the final inch, I sense my shoulder blades rip through my skin. My chest cavity opens, my ribs split apart and blood pools through my dress. I must be screaming but I'm not sure.

The Guardian is shouting but I can't hear what she says. Juliet is screaming. Alexei is crouched only two paces away, holding his head in his hands, paler than I ever expected to see him.

But there.

There.

I press my hand to Cain's chest, his soul's fragile flame warming my palm for a moment before it sinks into him, the glow spreading from my hand. It travels in every direction, up to his shoulders, his neck, his face, down to his lungs, his stomach, and beyond, where his armor conceals it.

He inhales, his chest rising and falling again. His eyes flash open, meeting mine.

I try to speak. I try to tell him that he is everything to me. But I have no air, nothing left, no more time. The room tips and my body sinks to his chest, my face turned to his.

My mind breaks.

CHAPTER TWENTY-ONE

"*D*on't move."

Alexei's voice reaches me through the fog inside my head. My thoughts swim, a mire of incoherent thoughts, the pain in my body beyond me. Too much to bear. The surface I'm resting on stops moving. Cain's broad chest. My head and shoulders rest against it, my hand pressed to his heart, my knees curled up beneath me pressed against his side. I am curled over him. I wish I could open my eyes but nothing responds to my wishes.

Cain's heartbeat thunders in my ears, and his distressed roar vibrates through my head. "Archer! No!"

I sense the agitated movement of his arms, his shoulders shifting, his torso rising beneath me. My pain shifts with him, the angles changing with every move he makes.

Alexei shouts, "Cain! Don't move or you'll break her."

"Break her? She's already broken." Cain's emotions crack. "Please tell me she's breathing."

Alexei's voice is really close, as if he's restraining Cain. He's also choosing his words. "She's ... alive. Juliet has gone to get Sarah and the medical team. You need to lie still until they tell us what to do."

"What the hell happened?

The Guardian's soft voice sounds from the other side. "Lady Tirelli killed you. I think we can safely assume that she controls a powerful assassin's ring that allows her to resist physical damage and makes her stronger. Your heart gave out after the fight with her. But then Archer..."

"What did she do?"

"She said she could save you. She was desperate to touch your chest, but it was like a force was pushing against her, and in the end her body..." The Guardian sucks in a sob. "Her body tore apart when she finally did it. That's when you woke up."

The silence fills only with Cain's heartbeats. Rapid. Like his breathing.

He whispers, "My soul. She gave me back my life."

There's a frown in the Guardian's voice. "What?"

Before Cain answers, multiple footsteps sound. I struggle again to open my eyes, concentrating as hard as I can until finally ... just barely ... I have the smallest slit of vision.

Sarah races toward me, kneeling swiftly. Her hands swill the space above my body without touching me.

Cain says, "Tell me you can help her."

Sarah shakes her head, her lips pursed. "Cain, I've never ... she's barely held together. Her back is ... it's a miracle she's still alive. This is far beyond my capabilities. I will use the magic in my ring to stabilize her, but I can't heal her. I'm sorry. There is no surgery for this."

Cain's roar echoes through the room. Alexei leans forward, his hands planted firmly on Cain's shoulders, muscles bunching, struggling to restrain him.

Sarah doesn't wait for a command, turning her attention back to me. Multiple gentle hands begin to work over me, the intermittent glow telling me that they are using their assassin's magic on me. Sarah murmurs while she works, her sporadic instructions to others indicating that a whole team is attempting to help me.

Alexei doesn't wait for Cain to calm down. "Cain, listen to me. We can't help Archer. None of us has that kind of healing power. But we all know who does."

Cain sucks in a sharp breath, grinding his response. "The Saber Lane Witch in Boston. The one who spelled my daggers. But that means taking Archer back into the heart of Legion Territory. I may as well deliver her to Slade!"

"No! There's another way." Alexei chews his words again. He casts a wary glance at the Guardian. "There's a way around the Code. But Cain ... you won't like it."

Cain shakes his head. "Don't test me, Alexei. I will do anything to save Archer, even fight Slade."

"What about giving her up?"

"What?"

Alexei says, "Slade can't touch Archer if she's an assassin. The hierarchy of rules in the Code will protect her."

Cain freezes and the Guardian sucks in a sharp breath, but Alexei plows on. "It would be unwise for me to train her, and even more so for you, Cain. Slade can't train her either. There is only one assassin who can take her on."

Alexei casts a demanding glare on the Guardian. "Will you sanction it, Guardian?"

The Guardian leans forward, worry and hope creasing her forehead. "If Archer is an assassin, then the fifth rule no longer applies to her—she is not a bystander anymore. The first rule will take priority." Her gentle eyes fill with emotion. "It's a stretch, but I believe the Code can accommodate it."

She lifts a stern finger. "On one condition. It must

be a clean start. Cain, if you agree to let Archer go, I will sanction her training as an assassin. Then she will be safe."

Cain closes his eyes. "You're telling me I have to put her out of my life. Send her to Boston to be healed. Never see her again."

Tears fill the Guardian's eyes. "I'm sorry, Cain. It's the only way this will work."

Cain sucks in a sharp breath, but his voice is dangerous. He turns his head to address each of the assassins. "Sarah, do not let Archer die. Juliet, you're my second in command now. Make sure the sentence on the remaining Novices is carried out."

I can't see Juliet, but her response is resolute. "Thank you, Master. The Novices are all dead."

"Good. I need you to arrange my jet to take Archer back to Boston. And ask Lutz to come in here, but without Parker. I don't want her to see this."

Moments later, powerful footsteps tell me that Lutz has joined us. He stops suddenly, barely entering my line of sight. The blood drains from his face. "Damn..."

I guess I must look pretty awful.

Cain's response is stern. "As soon as Archer is stabilized, you will take her to the Saber Lane Witch. Guardian, will you please explain?"

She says, "I have sanctioned Archer's training as an

assassin. She is no longer the Legion's target. I will inform Slade and travel with you to make sure the message is clear. We need to hurry. Archer doesn't have long."

Lutz cycles through surprise, to relief, to concern. He gives Cain a firm nod. "Understood. I promise you, Archer will arrive safely."

As he speaks, a figure appears behind him, slender and quiet. Parker is pale as she draws to a halt, her focus shifting from me to Cain. "Oh no ... Archer..."

"Parker." Lutz spins. I guess she snuck up on him again. He angles himself between her and me, attempting to block her view.

He says, "You were supposed to stay outside."

Fire enters her eyes. "Why? Because I can't handle it?" She paces right up to him, not letting him get in her way. "Archer is my friend too."

Lutz growls, "You don't need to see this kind of violence."

"Don't put me on a pedestal, Lutz Logan!"

His response is so quiet I almost miss it. "Innocence is worth protecting. You still have yours. Don't give it up so quickly."

She inhales. Exhales. The indignant fire in her eyes dies and the edges around her lips soften as she gazes back at him.

Cain contemplates them both. He says, "Lutz ... you have my permission to come back."

Lutz spins. "What?"

"You heard me."

"I—" Lutz swallows his gruff response. "Okay." He falls silent as Parker slips her hand into his. Her eyes fill with tears as she watches over me and Cain. She's the only one who isn't afraid to shed them.

Cain lets out his breath, but his focus becomes far away, as if he's folding up his true emotions and putting them in a safe place. A blank mask slowly takes their place. He lifts his left hand slowly, very carefully, toward my face. His focus shifts from the ring on his hand, the declaration he made with it, to my face, my lips.

He searches my eyes, whispering, "Archer? Can you hear me?"

I want to tell him so much, but I can't speak. My eyelids close, then open again, but barely. My heart is physically shattered, but this pain … is worse.

Cain brushes his thumb across my forehead, a gentle graze that is more powerful to me than the tear along my spine.

He says, "I'm going to use my magic to help you sleep now. But I promise you … you will be okay. I love you, Archer Ryan."

His assassin's ring glows and his face blurs. I fight the pull, the descending darkness, wanting to hold on to this last moment with him.

Against my will, I sink into oblivion.

~

I wake in an unfamiliar room, lying on an unfamiliar bed. The room is sparsely furnished with a closet and a bedside table, but nothing else. No lamp, no sharp objects, not even a blanket or sheets. I'm lying on a bare mattress, wearing sweatpants and a sweater that don't belong to me. They're soft and comfortable, I'll give them that. A book on the bedside table is the only thing I recognize. It's the book Lutz stabbed through—the one that saved my life.

A quick inventory of all my limbs tells me I am intact, pain free, my entire body responsive to my mind's commands. *I'm healed.* But as for where I am…

A woman leans against the far wall, about eight feet away. She is as tall as I am, casually dressed in jeans and a sleeveless shirt. Her mahogany hair sweeps long and free across one shoulder, her emerald eyes rimmed in silver. A tattoo adorns her right arm, but I can't make out the design from this angle.

She watches me carefully as she says, "I'm sorry about your surroundings, but I couldn't take the chance that you'd react before you let me speak."

My gaze flicks to the bedside table. "I could probably throw the book at you."

She smiles. It's surprisingly warm. Genuine. Carries the slightest hint of hope. "Cain said you were resourceful."

I try not to hurt at the sound of his name. "Where is he?"

She lifts herself off the wall, her smile fading, a deep sadness taking its place. "Where you left him. But certainly not where he wants to be."

I sit up and slide my legs over the edge of the bed, making no sudden movements, testing my strength. For now I'm prepared to listen. "Who are you?"

She says, "I'm Hunter Cassidy. Perhaps you've heard of me."

I nod. "I'm told nobody messes with you."

She levels her gaze with me. "Which is why nobody will mess with you now."

"And this place?"

"I live above a bookstore. I believe that might appeal to you."

It's impossible for me to hide the tiny spark of happiness I find in the darkness of my situation. I can escape into books. Books have happy endings. Books will always give me hope. Hope that no matter what happens, I will find a way back to Cain.

Hunter contemplates me with the quiet confidence of a woman who knows her own fears and has conquered all of them. She tips her chin at me, a spark of challenge entering her expression. "Are you willing to train with me and become an assassin, Archer Ryan?"

I find myself saying, "Yes."

Read more in Assassin's Maze.

ASSASSIN'S MAGIC 1

Is love worth the danger?

When Hunter Cassidy plans to infiltrate the Assassin's Legion, posing as an assassin-in-training, she is prepared to encounter danger every step of the way. What she doesn't expect is the ruggedly handsome and relentlessly fierce trainee, Slade Baines.

It's hard enough that Hunter is the first female to be accepted to train with the Master Assassin himself. Even when she beats the other candidates, the Master ranks her lowest of all. In the male-dominated Legion, the other trainees see her as a weak link to be driven out of their ranks.

Every time they try to force Hunter out, Slade gets in

their way, becoming an unexpected ally. Despite her best intentions, Hunter finds herself lowering her guard around him, which only makes carrying out her secret mission more difficult and puts her in danger of falling for him.

But there's more at stake than Hunter's heart. The Master Assassin possesses the key to locate a weapon that Hunter must ensure remains hidden at all costs.

In her quest to stop this deadly power from falling into the wrong hands, she must make a choice between following her heart... or fulfilling her destiny.

This is a full-length novel at 90,000 words, the first in the Assassin's Magic series.

Start the series with Assassin's Magic.

ASSASSIN'S MAGIC 2: ASSASSIN'S MASK

Is love worth fighting for?

When Hunter Cassidy revealed her true power to Slade Baines during a fight for their lives, everything she wanted was ripped away from her.

Now, with her heart in pieces, Hunter is left only with her determination to find and destroy the deadly weapon that led her to infiltrate the Assassin's Legion in the first place.

But Hunter's quest proves more complicated than she expected, leaving her with no choice but to make a deal with one of the Legion's most formidable assassins—a deal that catapults her right back into Slade's life.

Now the Master Assassin, Slade's power grows by the day and so does his determination to fight the bond he formed with Hunter and the powerful attraction that keeps drawing them together. No matter what, he will protect her from the enemies she makes at every turn, including the new leader of the underground whose mission is to destroy them both.

When tragedy strikes, Hunter discovers that the weapon she sought is nothing like she expected. She and Slade will need to work together to defeat the rising power behind the underground. But can they fight together when their hearts are torn apart?

Read more in Assassin's Mask.

ASSASSIN'S MAGIC 4: ASSASSIN'S MAZE

Can love survive?

When Hunter Cassidy exposed the true identity of the underground's brutal leader, she also uncovered the devastating truth about her own life.

With her time running out, Hunter must ally herself with her mortal enemy—the only woman with the power to destroy Hunter and everything she loves, including Slade Baines.

Determined not to lose Hunter, Slade will do anything to find the final Realm that holds the secret to saving Hunter and destroying their enemies once and for all.

But within the Realm is a maze of dangers, magical creatures of myth and legend, and a labyrinth of traps that will force Hunter and Slade to make deadly sacrifices, threatening their alliances, their lives... and their love.

Read more in Assassin's Maze.

ABOUT THE AUTHOR

Everly Frost is the USA Today Bestselling author of YA and New Adult urban fantasy and science-fiction romance novels. She spent her childhood dreaming of other worlds and scribbling stories on the leftover blank pages at the back of school notebooks. She lives in Brisbane, Australia with her husband and two children.

Join Everly's Immortal Legion (Reader Group)
https://www.facebook.com/
groups/247879889219423/

Join Everly's Mailing List:
http://www.everlyfrost.com/newsletter/

Please review! Reader reviews are an important part of a book's success by helping other readers discover stories they might enjoy. Please consider taking a moment to leave a review.

amazon.com/author/everlyfrost

facebook.com/everlyfrost

twitter.com/everlyfrost

instagram.com/everlyfrost

bookbub.com/authors/everly-frost

CPSIA information can be obtained
at www.ICGtesting.com
Printed in the USA
LVHW100111250922
729205LV00022B/422

ASSASSIN'S MENACE

Never step between an assassin and his prey.

Nobody would suspect bookworm Grace Kennedy of being a cold-blooded killer. She just wants to keep her head down and escape the violent secrets of her past.

But when Grace unwittingly gets between an assassin and his target, she becomes prey to Boston's most ferocious legion of killers.

If finding a way out of the life-threatening mess she created isn't hard enough, her unexpected encounters with Cain Carter prove even more unsettling.

Ruthless millionaire on the outside, sexy as hell in private, Cain is determined to make sure Grace survives her own secret power, as well as his.

When the Legion closes in and the power inside Grace threatens to tear her apart, Cain will have to sacrifice what he loves the most if he wants Grace to survive.

ISBN 978-0-6481948-4-2

90000

9 780648 194842